THE
OF DAR

A SPACE DETECTIVE
AGENCY ADVENTURE

SDA-V.1

MARTIN STREET

For my darling wife, Ali, who supports and loves me without question. And for my wonderful son, Jack, who came up with the name Eddie Poncho.

The dream is alive. I love you both.

CONTENTS

CHAPTER 1

'Three, two, one…'

The room suddenly filled with a high-pitched sound. The whole of Eddie Poncho's body tensed and his eyes widened. He tried to gather his thoughts and started to reach over to the silver box that was next to his left ear. As he turned his head, the bright green light illuminated his face and burned into his eyes. Eddie lifted his hand and shielded his face. His mind was already beginning to work overtime. It had been three months since the last green light and he knew exactly what it meant: Mossop would be here in five and he wouldn't be getting any sleep for a while.

Eddie reached over to the box and within moments of placing his hand over the beam of light the room fell silent. He felt his body began to relax. He closed his eyes, took a big deep breath and held it.

And held it… and held it.

And then, just as his lungs began to tingle, he breathed out until the lightness in his head disappeared. His mind was now completely clear and he felt ready for Mossop. Experience had taught him that he needed to be in complete control when his friend arrived. Mossop got a bit over-excited when things went Green Alert and it wouldn't help if he was in the same state.

Four clicks before his tranquil apartment descended into complete chaos: Eddie just about had time for a hyper-shower and a glass of Baboo. He reached up to the panel above his head, touched the orange button and prepared himself for the fine mist that was about to engulf him. He whispered, 'Froo zest,' and waited for the distinctive smell to fill his nostrils. Nothing was quite as refreshing as a froo zest hyper-shower, except maybe a froo bar, but they were only sold on Dar these days.

Two clicks until Mossop…

Eddie strapped up his boots, jumped to his feet

and walked to the chiller. He grabbed the carton of Baboo from the shelf inside the chiller's door and poured himself a large glass. 'I wonder what today has in store,' he said to himself, before downing the liquid in one. He looked at the empty glass, and then looked up at the door to the apartment. Eddie's face broke into a broad grin. It was almost time. He placed a second glass next to his and filled both with the remains of the Baboo. Then, in one swift movement, he turned 180 degrees and launched the empty carton across the room. 'Bingo!' Eddie shouted, as the carton disappeared into the rubbish chute by the chiller. He pumped his fist in celebration and walked over to the door.

'Three, two, one…'

The door disappeared and there stood Mossop Yate, the only Quagoid on Parsus.

The two friends greeted each other in the traditional Parsian way, by showing the palms of their hands before speaking. Eddie knew that Mossop would be bursting to speak and was happy for him to let rip. 'Have you had a glass of Baboo yet, Eddie?' Mossop asked.

Eddie nodded at the glass on the table and said, 'That's my second. The other's ready and waiting for you.' Mossop was nervous and edgy.

'Good,' Mossop replied. 'You're going to need it.'

Eddie frowned. Just for a moment, he was concerned. He'd expected Mossop to arrive in his usual state of excitement and high agitation. He'd grab his glass of Baboo and chuck it down his neck as fast as he could. That's how it was when they were given a new job. But this was different. Mossop was quiet and subdued. The two friends had grown up together and in all that time, Eddie could only remember a handful of occasions when the Quagoid looked as serious as he did right now.

Mossop walked over to the table, picked up the glass and gulped down half of the Baboo. He gave the half-empty glass to Eddie and walked over to the window, his shoulders slumped. Eddie couldn't contain himself any longer: 'What is it, Mossop? Is it a job?'

Mossop waved his hand in front of the window. As the window disappeared he felt the chill of the night air on his face. He looked out across the skyline and then up into the cloudless, purple sky. 'Dar looks bright,' he said, thoughtfully. 'I'm not sure I fancy living in the sky for the rest of my life.'

Eddie was getting impatient now and was beginning to think that his friend had completely lost the plot. 'Mossop, what is it?' he asked in a stern voice. 'Why are we on green?'

Mossop turned to face Eddie and, with a look of horror on his face, said, 'The Gems of Dar have gone!'

There was a large crash as the glass slipped from Eddie's hand and hit the floor. Shards of glass, mixed with the thick, blue Baboo were thrown across the floor of the apartment, not to mention Eddie's boots. Eddie stood, rooted to the spot, his mouth and eyes wide open. He was suddenly conscious that his whole body had tensed, and his heart was thumping so hard he thought it was going to burst through his chest. He was barely breathing and yet his breath seemed as loud as his heartbeat. Then, as if waking from a trance, he blinked his eyes and gulped deeply before whispering, 'Gone? Gone where?'

Mossop looked down at mess on the floor and replied, without raising his head, 'Someone has taken them.'

Eddie heard the words but, somehow, they just didn't sink in. Mossop had still not raised his head from the mess on the floor. He hadn't thought beyond this point. It had taken all of his strength just to say those words, and he had no plan for what he was going to say or do next. Finally, he raised his head and looked into Eddie Poncho's wet eyes. He took a deep breath and said, 'Someone has taken the Gems of Dar.'

Even though no other words had passed between them, Eddie and Mossop both fully understood the significance of what had happened.

The Gems of Dar were the only reason they were there at all. The gems are rare and almost impossible to find. They are known as one of the most precious minerals in the universe and have the power to create and sustain life. In ancient times, the Darian Palace used them to create the Darian Light, a powerful energy field that crossed space as far as Dar's neighbouring planet, Parsus. As the population of Dar grew, so the planet's resources became less and less. Given its distance from the Qenos System's star, Parsus was little more than a toxic piece of rock, covered in a mixture of hot gas and fire; it was completely uninhabitable. The Darian Royal Family's dream was to create two planets with the same life-giving atmosphere. New homes that would create food for Darians but would also give new life to the fireball planet.

It took two generations to build the Darian Light. Once it was completed, five gems, which had been excavated in a remote mining town and stored in the vaults of the Royal Palace, were placed in the Light's Spectral Chamber. The gems were the precious key that provided enough energy to recreate Dar's life-giving atmosphere on Parsus.

Dar was a peaceful planet and had no wish to turn its neighbour into Dar #2. Once the atmosphere on Parsus had allowed life to start evolving, and had created a sustainable ecosystem, Darians were allowed to settle on it. As the years passed, all manner of animal, plant and human life was created. Parsians were born and Darian settlers had children and grandchildren of their own. Over the following one thousand years, Darian kings and queens came and went but the philosophy remained the same. Each planet developed its own cultures and civilisations but, dependent upon each other for their very existence, both lived in perfect peace and harmony.

And so, for a thousand years, the planets of Dar and Parsus had peacefully co-existed. This history was so important to Darians and Parsians that everyone understood it. It was written in the Ancient Laws: without the gems, there was no Darian Light and without the Light, there was no Parsus and, ultimately, no Dar. Everyone knew this.

CHAPTER 2

'We haven't got much time.'

Eddie and Mossop stepped onto the escalator and began their journey up to the imposing entrance of the Space Detective Agency's Command Centre. Eddie looked across to Mossop and stared deeply into his friend's big black eyes. Mossop blinked his eyes from side to side and allowed himself a nervous smile. As they neared the top of the escalator, the top of a head appeared... then a mane of white hair... the piercing blue eyes... that beard... the broad shoulders. Commander Max Ramad, the respected chief of the Space Detective Agency had come down from his office to meet the two young agents. Ramad's arms moved from behind his back. He held his huge hands out in front of his body before placing one on Eddie's shoulder and one of Mossop's. 'I'm sorry to have recalled you so soon, boys,' he whispered. 'You'll be leaving in an hour… we haven't got much time.'

Eddie and Mossop followed their leader through the SDA's grand entrance and stepped into the security curtain: a beam of white light that spread across the width of the entrance. They walked over to one of the hyper-plates and stepped on it. In his still-hushed tone, Ramad said, 'Control,' and within seconds the lift had arrived at its destination.

Ramad walked purposefully over to the glass-screened area in the corner of the room and sat at his desk. As he did so, he pointed to the chairs on the other side of the table. The boys sat down.

Ramad stroked his beard and began his briefing. 'This is what we know. Two hours ago, a group calling themselves the *Children of Zomak* entered the Darian Royal Palace and made their way to the Spectral Chamber. At the moment, we don't know how they managed to access the chamber but they knew how to deactivate the beam, open the inner

chamber and extract the five gems. Then they just…'
Ramad suddenly stopped talking, as if the magnitude
of what he'd just told Eddie and Mossop had hit him
like a hungry Kaarbu warrior.

'They just… what?' Eddie prompted. Ramad
didn't answer. Suddenly, he seemed lost in a world of
his own. Eddie tried again: 'Sir!' No reply.

'Commander, what did they do?' Mossop urged.

Max Ramad was a hard man, who'd seen too many
bad things in his life. His laser-blue eyes stared
straight ahead, his voice was steady. 'All of the
technicians are accounted for,' he said quietly, 'but the
group have put them in some kind of trance or
they've frozen their brains or something. To be
honest, we don't really know what they've done to
them. They're still in the Spectral Chamber, floating
in some kind of stasis, and we can't speak to any of
them until it wears off, if it ever does. But it might be
too late by then.'

Ramad brought himself out of his own trance, as if
the emotional shield he'd erected was no longer
required. Like the true spy he was, it was back to
business.

'Boys, we have two days,' he continued. 'The Light
has gone out. Parsus will start to die quickly and will

be dead as a planet unless the gems are found and reinstalled inside the Spectral Chamber. We've started working on the evacuation plan. Go to your Star Jumper and get it kitted out for field operations. You'll need some local help. We have a contact there: a very special young woman, as you'll soon discover. I'll update you before you make the jump to Dar. Questions?'

Eddie had one. 'What do we know about this group, the *Children of Zomak*? I've never heard of them.'

Ramad stroked his white beard. 'We have a message from them. You'll see on the shuttle. Any more questions?' Eddie and Mossop both shook their heads. 'OK, then. Go and get ready.'

CHAPTER 3

'We are watching...

we are waiting...'

As Mossop guided the Star Jumper through Parsus' outer sphere, Eddie completed preparations for the jump to Dar. Once the co-ordinates were programmed in, he turned to Mossop and said, 'Right, let's find out what this is all about.' Mossop could sense the tension in his old friend's voice. He felt it too but gave a reassuring nod and smile. The two young space detectives had worked on enough cases together to understand the importance of keeping their emotions in check, even if the very existence of their planet relied on this mission being a complete success.

Eddie took a deep breath and exhaled slowly. 'Commander Ramad, we're ready…' he said.

Ramad's face appeared on the screen and his steely voice filled the flight deck. 'OK boys, this is it. We received this transmission two hours ago. First, listen. Questions after.'

Ramad's face was replaced by a large green 'Z'. Eddie and Mossop looked at each other. What the hell was this? They looked back at the screen, just in time to see the image change from the large luminous letter to an image of the Spectral Chamber's technicians floating in stasis. Mossop's large black eyes blinked from side to side as the camera shot panned around the chamber. One after another, the bodies of the technicians appeared until the shot finally came to a standstill. As the camera zoomed in on the trance-like face of a young female technician, the silence was broken with a voice that made the hairs on the back of Eddie's neck stand on end.

'We are the Children of Zomak.

'On this day, 10 long years ago, the Darians sent our family into exile on the prison planet of Cabor. After years of faithful and loyal service, our beloved father, the mighty Tak Zomak, was found guilty of treason. Condemned without trial,

and denied every Darian's right to speak for themselves, he was labelled a traitor. The family of Zomak were banished from their home planet for life and left to rot.

'But Tak was innocent.

'It is Brude, the so-called "People's King" who is the treacherous one. You betrayed our father, who loved you as a brother and would have sacrificed his own life to save you or any member of the Royal Family. We are Darians by birth, but today is the first day of the death of Dar and the parasite planet Parsus.

'For your crimes against our family, we have taken the Gems of Dar from the Spectral Chamber. As the Ancient Laws decree, without the life-giving light of the gems, Parsus will be dead in two days. As Parsus reaches the day of its death, Zero Day, its inhabitants will flee to Dar. This will cause chaos and decay to hit Dar.

'This is your legacy, Brude: the quick death of Parsus and the slow, more painful death of Dar. That will be our victory. But, there is a way to save Dar.

'In return for passing control of Dar to the Children of Zomak, we will allow safe passage of the Royal Family to Parsus. Once the Royal Family has landed, they will be allowed to live out their days. We will then return the gems to the Spectral Chamber before taking our place on the throne. As for Parsus, as a reminder of the crimes of Brude, the Darian

14

Light will be switched off at sunset on the first day of our reign and darkness will fall on Dar once more. At sunset on the second day, the Light will be switched back on. And so it will continue. Parsus will remain in a constant state of decay whilst Dar is ruled by the Children of Zomak.

'For every hour that passes before the Darian Light returns, Parsus will take longer to regenerate to its current state of evolution.

'You condemned our family to the dark abyss of the prison planet Cabor. Now, King Brude, the clock is ticking for your family and for the people of Dar and Parsus.

'We are watching…

'We are waiting…'

The emotionless face of the young technician was replaced by a giant green 'Z' and silence descended on the flight deck once more.

Ramad's face reappeared on the screen. 'OK, boys,' he said, 'make the jump to Dar's outer sphere. Mossop, you're a student of your planet's history: start thinking about anything that can help us. I'll update you on what we know once you hit Dar.'

Mossop ran the final systems check and turned to face his friend. 'Ready to jump, Eddie?' he asked with a smile. This was already shaping up to be their most dangerous mission but Eddie and Mossop could still feel the adrenaline rush that came with every jump. The Space Detective Agency was on the case and the space detectives were on their way. Adventures in the stars, it was what they lived for. Eddie's face broke into a huge grin and Mossop knew exactly what was coming next.

Eddie raised his right arm above his head and pointed his forefinger. Then, he threw his arm forwards towards the front of the flight deck, pointed at the stars, and screamed, 'Juuuuuuuuuuuump!' Mossop hit the hyper-jump button and the Star Jumper cut through space.

Next stop: Dar.

CHAPTER 4

'I can't believe this has anything to do with him.'

As the Star Jumper settled into its journey, Eddie and Mossop had a bit of time to reflect on what had been a hectic couple of hours. Mossop checked the flight stabilisers one last time and leant back in his chair. 'The Children of Zomak…' he wondered out loud.

'The what?' Eddie replied with a quizzical look on his face. Mossop put his hands behind his head and began to swivel his chair from side to side. He repeated himself, safe in the knowledge that he now had Eddie's attention. 'The Children of Zomak,' he said, 'I was just thinking about them.'

Eddie had been thinking about the trance-like expression on the face of the young technician. He couldn't get the image of her face out of his mind. He felt a bit in the dark and needed to be analysing the evidence, working out a plan. He was keen to start talking about the mission.

'I've never heard of them,' he replied. 'What's on your mind?'

'Zomak's a pretty historical name back on Zota,' Mossop said. The Quagoid was warming to his theme and had started swivelling his chair faster.

'Really?' said Eddie. 'How do you mean? Is it a place?'

'No,' said Mossop. 'Not a place, a person. He's was a bit of a legend, actually. He was a soldier from Dar, a young captain in the Darian Guard. During the Praal Uprising 30 years ago, he led a joint unit of Zotans and Darians that launched a surprise attack on the compound of the Praal warlord.'

Eddie interrupted, 'Praal?'

Mossop continued as though Eddie hadn't spoken. 'The Praals are a warrior race from the south of Zota. They fought alongside Kaarbu in the War of Sighs.

They're fierce, fighting's what they do. I tell you, back in the day, if you were going to face the Praals you better be ready because they didn't take prisoners.'

Eddie interrupted again. 'Didn't?'

Mossop looked at Eddie and said, 'What?'

'You said didn't.'

'Oh,' said Mossop, 'they don't fight anymore. When Zota defeated the Kaarbu, they signed the peace treaty. They mine a precious underwater mineral that's used in medicine.' Mossop sighed, which made Eddie smile. 'Anyway, 30 years ago, the Praal decided that they could no longer live under the rule of Kaarbu and made an attempt on the throne of Zota. Their warlord was camped on the edge of the city and Zomak led the assault to attack him. The King of Dar, Ath II, personally authorised the attack.

'When Zomak's elite unit burst in on the Praal leadership, they were planning their final attack on the capital. Zomak captured them all and became an instant hero. He pretty much saved Zota.'

Mossop had stopped swinging on his chair and was beginning to look worried. Eddie had been listening carefully. His friend had a knack for identifying crucial facts in their investigations and he wasn't about to start putting obstacles in the way.

'That's some story, Mossop,' he eventually said.

Mossop leant forwards and checked the stabilisers. 'We'll be coming out of the jump in two minutes' time,' he said.

Eddie had begun to formulate some more questions. 'Where is Zomak now?' he asked.

Mossop's answer went some way to explaining why he had begun to look so worried. 'Well, that's just it,' he replied. 'When he went back to Dar, he was appointed commander of the Darian Royal Family's personal guard. I mean, he wasn't just responsible for their protection, he became their friend. He was loved by everyone who served under him and really, he was more like the king's personal advisor. As you know, Dar is a very open society.' Eddie nodded in agreement, encouraging Mossop to continue. 'Well, as time went on, I think Zomak forgot that first and foremost he was there to protect the Royal Family. Then, one day, 10 years ago, the queen was kidnapped by the new Praal warlord.'

Mossop fell silent for a few seconds before turning to face Eddie. 'She was never found…' he said quietly.

Eddie sat in stunned silence. His mind was working overtime but his train of thought was broken by the signal that they were about to exit the jump.

Mossop started to prepare the Star Jumper for its approach to the spaceport, whilst Eddie got ready to contact Commander Ramad.

Mossop took his eyes off the flight screen for a moment and glanced at Eddie. 'Ramad told me to think about the history of Zota. Zomak is a big part of it.' Mossop shook his head and puffed out his cheeks. 'I can't believe this has anything to do with him, though,' he said.

CHAPTER 5

'She's our hidden treasure. We keep her very secret.'

Max Ramad's booming voice echoed around the Star Jumper's flight deck. 'So, Mossop, I assume you've told Eddie all about Tak Zomak?'

Eddie and Mossop looked at each other before Mossop's head dropped. 'Please tell me he's not involved in this, sir,' he said.

'We're not sure,' came the reply, 'but we think his children are. I don't know how much Mossop has told you, Eddie, but I don't have time to give you any more information, I'm needed here. We can't contain this thing for long and it's going to be chaos here soon. People will be crawling over each other to get away from this planet. Get to the spaceport on Dar as quickly as you can. Our Darian agent will meet you there and take you straight to the Spectral Chamber. I'll be keeping up-to-date with her whilst you're making the jump.'

Eddie raised his eyebrows in surprise. 'We have an agent on Dar?' he asked, feeling somewhat out of the loop.

'We do,' Ramad replied with a slightly crooked smile. 'You didn't know that, did you?' Mossop smiled. Eddie liked to think he knew about everything that went on at the SDA, but he sometimes forgot that he worked for a secret organisation!

'Our space detective on Dar is Stelvina,' Ramad said. As he said her name, Stelvina's face replaced Ramad's on the screen. 'She's been working with us for the last five years,' he continued.

'Never heard of her!' Eddie snorted, betraying his sense of being miffed at not knowing something so important about the Space Detective Agency. Ramad didn't have time to stroke Eddie's ego and chose to ignore his mildly aggressive tone. 'You won't have, she's our hidden treasure. We keep her very secret.'

Mossop was intrigued by Stelvina's file image. She had long white hair and big emerald green eyes. The same colour, Mossop imagined, as the Gems of Dar. 'Why do you keep her secret from the other agents, sir?' he inquired.

'Ah, the golden question, Mossop. You both have your talents and Stelvina's no different. She has a very special gift that we wouldn't want to fall into the wrong hands.'

Ramad's gruff voice became notably softer.

'Stelvina has the ability to ultra-empathise with her surroundings. She can completely blend in with them. In fact, she can do this so effectively that she disappears. She becomes at one with her immediate environment.'

'Invisible…' Eddie said quietly, almost to himself.

'Exactly,' Ramad responded. 'That's how she appears, or rather doesn't! But there's a price. Blending sucks her energy and leaves her feeling extremely weak. In fact, it leaves her so weak that she can only blend for a short period of time and only in situations where she'll be completely safe when she releases herself. If she blends for too long, she loses consciousness and immediately returns to her natural state. Of course, the irony is that as a space detective, she generally only needs to blend in potentially dangerous situations. It's a great but very hazardous gift. I'm sure *you* can empathise with that, Mossop?'

Mossop blinked his eyes from side to side. 'Yes, sir, I can.'

Commander Max Ramad's voice became stern once more. 'Right, I've got a queue of people here and they're all fighting for my attention, so one last thing,' he said, returning to his focus its usual gruff efficiency. 'Stelvina was born in the mining town of Mount Sukat. It's where the gems were excavated a thousand years ago. It's a source of great pride to the town. For her this is personal. Now, get to the spaceport. Stelvina will meet you there.'

CHAPTER 6

'Do you consider yourself cursed, Quagoid?'

Mossop expertly guided the Star Jumper to landing bay #6 and sought final clearance from Flight Control to land at the spaceport. Three legs appeared from the Star Jumper's under-body and it gently bounced as it landed. 'Welcome to Dar,' said the voice from Flight Control. 'We're glad you're here and wish you a successful mission... for all our sakes.'

Eddie responded with a short but genuine, 'Thank you, we'll do our best,' before switching off the communications link.

As he got out of his chair, Mossop tapped him on the arm and nodded towards the front of the Star Jumper: 'Our liaison?' he queried.

Eddie looked up and saw the lonely figure standing in the entrance of the loading bay. He could see the young woman's pale face but her hair was hidden beneath the hood of the white gown that was gently billowing in the evening breeze. He looked at Mossop and smiled. 'I guess so.'

Eddie and Mossop grabbed their packs from the small storage area and stood on the Jumper's entrance ramp. Mossop touched the screen and the ramp descended. As they emerged into the bright light of loading bay #6 they were greeted by the white figure. Whilst they were collecting their packs, Stelvina had walked to the front of the Jumper and was now standing next to its front leg.

She pulled the hood from her head, allowing her long white hair to fall over her shoulders. For the first time, her emerald green eyes were visible. Mossop's eyes blinked from side to side. 'Stelvina?' Eddie enquired.

'Yes,' came the reply. 'And you're Eddie Poncho. Code name: Fire. You've been a space detective for five years. You graduated first in your class, having recorded the highest ever score in the academy's leadership test. This is your 10th mission and your special…'

Eddie put his hand up and interrupted, 'OK, that'll do. You seem to know a lot about me?' he said, in a questioning tone. Stelvina smiled just enough for Eddie to notice, but she ignored his question and looked across to Mossop.

'Mossop Yate!' she said. Mossop clenched his teeth tightly. The two young space detectives stood staring at each other in silence for a few seconds. Mossop blinked his big eyes, preparing himself for Stelvina's 'Guide to Mossop' but the young woman didn't say anything.

The silence was beginning to get a bit awkward and it was Eddie who spoke first. 'And…?' he asked, annoyed that Mossop was being spared the Stelvina treatment.

Stelvina's smile had vanished and she now looked faintly sad. 'Is it true?' she said finally.

Mossop frowned. 'Is what true?' he replied.

Stelvina sighed heavily. She would have to answer her own question. 'Mossop Yate,' she said, 'the only Quagoid on Parsus. Do you consider yourself cursed, Quagoid?'

Eddie took a sharp intake of breath. Mossop was quite capable of looking after himself but Stelvina's introduction technique was beginning to irritate him. 'Alright, Stelvina,' he said, 'I think that's…'

Mossop held his hand out as he interrupted his friend. 'No problem, Eddie,' he said, maintaining eye contact with Stelvina. 'It's an interesting philosophical question. Do I feel cursed? I could ask you the same question, Stelvina,' he said. Eddie's smile did not go unnoticed by Stelvina. 'We Quagoids do not think that way,' Mossop continued. He was beginning to enjoy this little duel with the Darian space detective and wanted to play her at her own game. 'You see, it's what we are, it's all we know. What some might call our curse, we call our gift. So to answer your question, no, I do not consider myself cursed. But like all Quagoids, my gift is not easily given.' Eddie allowed himself a little chuckle. Mossop had played it beautifully.

Stelvina nodded her head in appreciation of Mossop's words. She had much more to say on the subject but there were more pressing matters. She decided to adopt a more friendly tone and held her hands out in the traditional Parsian greeting. 'Let us hope that we can get through this crisis without either of us having to use our special gift,' she said, in an attempt to soften the atmosphere.

'I fear that won't be possible,' Mossop replied but was happy to leave this particular conversation... for the time being at least.

'Now, please,' Stelvina motioned towards the loading bay's entrance, 'follow me to the Spectral Chamber. There's something I need to show you.'

As Stelvina turned and walked towards the entrance, the lads looked at each other and smiled. This was going to be an interesting few days.

CHAPTER 7

'I remember the day they came

for us.'

Rok Zomak sat staring at the five green gems that were lined up in front of her. Looking at them now, as the sun began to set, it was difficult to believe that they were responsible for having created life on another planet. She leant over her crossed legs, picked up the middle gem and held it up to the shimmering orange disk that was on its rapid journey towards the horizon. The sun still had enough power to enter the centre of the gem, a tiny orange light trapped in a sea of green. Rok felt hypnotised by its beauty. The sun's last warmth seemed to be flickering inside the gem. 'Beautiful, aren't they?' Bak nodded at his sister as he reached across her shoulder and plucked the gem from her hand. Bak weighed the gem in his hand. It wasn't as heavy as it looked.

The older Zomak looked up at the sun, which was about to disappear behind a huge mountain. 'We can't stay here for much longer,' he whispered quietly, almost to himself.

'I know,' Rok replied.

Bak placed his hand gently on his younger sister's shoulder. 'They'll be getting organised now,' he said, 'and this is the first place they'll come to.' He turned and looked at the remains of the villa where they were born.

Rok stood up. 'I don't remember much about living here, do you?' she asked.

Bak walked over to the hole where the front door used to be and held his hand out, as if he was touching an imaginary door. 'I remember the day they came for us,' he said, again in a whisper. 'You know, it was the worst day of my life. Mama was screaming and you were so scared. I don't think you understood what was happening but because Mama was so upset, that made you upset.' Rok wanted to say something but couldn't find the right words so she let Bak continue. 'They wanted to take Papa away from us,' he continued, 'but the Captain was a friend of Papa's. They'd served together on Zota. Papa spoke with him and the Captain agreed to go against his orders and let us all leave together, as a family. If he hadn't agreed to that, I think that would have been the last time we saw Papa.'

Rok had now joined her brother at the empty doorway and looked up at him. She could see that his eyes were wet and that he was fighting to hold back the tears. 'Weren't you scared?' she asked.

Bak turned to face her. 'Of course,' he replied, 'but Papa asked me to help you and Mama so I tried to be strong. I wanted to show Papa that I could be brave, that he could rely on me to look after you both. It was really hard. I didn't know what was going to happen, and I didn't know where they were going to take us. I think Papa knew, though.'

Bak looked up at the black sky, which was already beginning to fill with bright, twinkling stars. 'They'll be here soon. We need to get moving.' Bak gave the gem back to his sister. 'Put the gems back in the transportation case and let's head to the city,' he said before walking over to the power-bike that was parked next to their old climbing wall.

Rok walked back over to the four remaining gems and placed the one she was holding in the centre of the transportation case. In an unexpected act of ceremony, she gently touched the gem closest to her. She paused for a moment and frowned before continuing around the case in a clockwise direction. As she reached each new corner she gently touched the gem, finishing with the one in the centre. She glanced back at her older brother before turning her attention back to the five gems, which she began to stare at.

Bak had walked past the bike and was now standing in front of the climbing wall. He stroked its rough surface and smiled. 'Hey, Rok,' he said, turning around to look at his sister. 'Do you remember the time we…?' but his little sister was busy with the transportation case. He turned back to face the wall. In his mind's eye, he pictured a scene of he and Rok climbing the wall 10 years ago. He allowed himself another smile and grabbed his helmet from the seat of the bike.

The silent night air was broken by the high-pitched whine of the power-bike starter. Bak flicked the generator button and the powerful engine roared into life. As it did so, it startled Rok, breaking her out of her trance. She gently closed the case, walked over, opened the storage compartment at the back of the bike and carefully placed it inside. She put on the other helmet, slung her leg over the bike and patted the back of the silver helmet in front of her. Bak Zomak pulled back on the handlebars and the bike sped off towards the city.

CHAPTER 8

'I don't think it's occurred to anyone that they might be stolen.'

Eddie and Mossop followed Stelvina past the two heavily armed guards into the brightly lit tunnel. As they walked to the end of the windowless corridor, Stelvina pointed ahead and said, 'We'll take the magic carpet from here.' As they came to the end of the corridor, Stelvina stopped and, with a swish of her right hand, invited the boys to step onto the shiny hyper-plate. Stelvina joined them and waved her hand against the dark screen on the wall. As she did so, the three young space detectives shot skywards. Their journey lasted only a matter of seconds before the plate came to a sudden, yet effortless stop at the top of the shaft. 'The penthouse suite,' she smiled. As she stepped off the plate, Stelvina pointed left, towards the only door in what was a much shorter corridor than the one on the ground floor. 'The entrance to the chamber is over there,' she said.

Eddie stepped off the plate and followed Stelvina. Mossop took the opportunity to look out of the small window at the top of the shaft. He couldn't quite believe what he saw. They were on the hyper-plate for just a few seconds but it looked like they were in the clouds. The twinkling lights of the city were far below them. 'Impressive,' Mossop mumbled to no-one in particular. He stepped off the plate and walked towards Eddie and Stelvina, who were now standing by the entrance to the Spectral Chamber.

Eddie was beginning to get impatient. He had watched the Zomaks' message and he'd listened to Mossop's potted history of the Zomak family, but he couldn't understand how they'd been able to steal the gems in the first place. 'So, Stelvina,' he said, slightly abruptly, 'how did they get up here and into the chamber?'

Stelvina could sense Eddie's impatience. She was

already thinking about what was waiting for them on the other side of the door and had allowed herself to become distracted. She responded quickly to Eddie Poncho's question. 'I spoke to Commander Ramad whilst you were flying here. We're working on the theory that the Zomaks had help on the inside.'

Mossop blinked his large black eyes from side to side. 'You mean someone who had a relationship with the Zomak family?' he asked.

Stelvina nodded. 'Yeah, it could be. That's what we're thinking, but we have no idea who.'

Mossop nodded in agreement. 'It's a good theory. How do we go about finding this person, though?'

Eddie wasn't convinced. 'OK,' he said, 'maybe they did have help. As Mossop says, that's a good place to start our investigation, but they still had to get up here and, having removed the gems from the chamber, had to get out again. This place must be the most guarded building in the solar system.'

It was more of a statement than a question but Stelvina looked down at the floor, not answering. After a few awkward seconds of silence, Eddie frowned. 'Stelvina?' he said, impatiently.

'You would think so, wouldn't you?' came Stelvina's quiet reply. Both Eddie and Mossop looked at each other and frowned, confused by her answer. Stelvina looked up, her emerald green eyes shining brightly in the corridor's white light. 'The Darian Light has been shining on Parsus for a thousand years,' Stelvina continued. 'Of course, we all know about Zero Day, but generations have grown up with the Light just being there. I don't think it's occurred to anyone that they might be stolen.'

Eddie was getting very concerned and was having trouble hiding his growing anger. 'I'm not sure I understand what you're saying, Stelvina,' he said, abruptly. Stelvina looked downwards at the floor once more. Mossop stepped forwards and gently placed an arm on one of Stelvina's slender shoulders. 'What is it?' he asked, quietly.

She looked up at Mossop, embarrassed by what she was about to say. She took a deep breath and, trying to sound as confident as she could, turned her gaze towards Eddie. 'What I'm saying, Poncho, is that there wasn't any security. The gems were unguarded.' Eddie and Mossop both stood there in silence, barely able to take in what Stelvina had just said. She continued. 'Of course, there's lots of security now, obviously. But before the gems were stolen, there were usually just a couple of guards downstairs.'

Mossop was the first to react. 'Usually?'

'I know, I know,' Stelvina responded. 'It's hard to believe. I was shocked myself. You know, it's all peace and quiet here. They just had no reason to think there was ever a danger of anything happening. I guess they just took things for granted.' Stelvina paused for a second before adding, 'They just got lazy. We all did.'

Eddie shook his head in disgust. He knew that this had nothing to do with Stelvina but, through their 'laziness', the Darian Royal Family had put millions of lives at risk and threatened the existence of two planets.

Mossop had been thinking and had a question. 'What about the kidnap?' he asked.

'Kidnap?' Stelvina asked, in reply.

'Yes. When the queen was kidnapped 10 years ago. Wasn't the security increased then? I mean, surely that was enough to make the Royal Family realise they couldn't just sit around leaving the whole planet unprotected?'

Stelvina was beginning to feel as though the two agents were holding her personally responsible for the gems being stolen. 'Look,' she said, her voice now trembling, 'there's no point interrogating me about the lack of security. Maybe none of this would be happening, maybe it would. But it *has* happened, and no amount of arguing about the lack of security is going to help us find either the gems or the Zomaks. Believe me, I'm as angry as anyone. Those gems were mined in my village 1,000 years ago. They're part of me, part of who I am and I'm going to get them back, if it's the last thing I do. Do you understand that?'

Both Eddie and Mossop knew that Stelvina was right. There would be a time for looking into that and it wasn't now. 'OK, OK,' said Eddie, trying to calm things down.

'Look, this isn't aimed at you.' Stelvina smiled weakly. 'I don't know any more about how they got in,' she insisted. 'Commander Ramad is looking into the theory of an insider.' She paused, aware that her skin had started to feel cold. She continued, almost in a whisper. 'But I do know what lies behind that door. And you need to see it…'

CHAPTER 9

'I'm Mossop. I'm here to help you.'

The door to the Spectral Chamber swished open and revealed the horrible scene inside. The frozen bodies of the 10 technicians hung in the air, as if suspended from the chamber's ceiling by some invisible rope. Their arms and legs were stiff and pointed towards the floor at an angle away from their bodies. The fingers on their hands were parted in the same way, spread out and separated from the one next to it, and their heads were pushed back as far as the neck could possibly go without snapping. The body of each technician was surrounded by a shimmering, blue haze that seemed to imprison them.

The technicians were floating at head height, their bodies hanging in the air. It gave them an appearance of relaxation but closer inspection showed that they were anything but relaxed. Their features were tight and they looked like they'd been unexpectedly hit by some force that had sent their bodies into a spasm and immediately frozen them.

It was a deeply disturbing scene.

Stelvina reached out to one of them. As she did so, a sharp electrical charge shot up her arm causing an involuntary reaction that made her pull it away from the floating figure in front of her. 'Ow!' she yelped, in some pain. As she began to rub her own arm, the pale blue haze that was formed around the technician's entire body began to crackle and fizz, as though it were alive. It shimmered for a few seconds before stopping just as suddenly as it had started. As the crackling stopped, the blue haze returned to the same state as with the other technicians.

'Curious,' said Eddie.

Mossop walked over to the technician that was closest to him and looked up at her face. It was an agonising sight. Her mouth was open and her jaw was tight, as if her face had been pulled back from her ears. Her eyes were shut so tightly that little creases had appeared at the corners of her closed eyelids. She looked in terrible pain. Mossop wanted to see again what happened when the strange blue light was touched.

'This is who we saw on the Zomaks' message. Alexa Karel, Communications Officer,' he whispered, reading the badge on her uniform. His right hand reached out towards Alexa's left hand but before it got to the blue light he stopped and said, as reassuringly as he could, 'I'm Mossop. I'm here to help you, Alexa.'

He took a deep breath and allowed his hand to continue its journey. He gently reached through the haze and touched the young woman's hand. There was a loud fizzing sound as the light slowly began to make its way up Mossop's arm. The Quagoid tilted his head to one side and blinked his eyes. He wanted to know what would happen if he maintained the connection. He gritted his teeth as the pain became more and more intense. Eddie walked over and gave his friend a concerned look. Mossop's jaw was beginning to tighten and his arm was shaking.

'Mossop,' Eddie commanded, 'let go now!'

The blue light had continued to travel up Mossop's arm. It was now at his shoulder but Mossop seemed completely unaware. 'Mossop,' Eddie shouted again, but his friend was locked in, trapped by the same power that had captured the chamber's technicians. Suddenly, Mossop's arm shot towards the ceiling of the chamber. As it did so, the blue light crackled and disappeared from Mossop's arm. Eddie looked at Stelvina, who had leapt in front of him and pushed Mossop's arm away from Alexa's body. Eddie smiled. 'Quick thinking,' he said.

Stelvina smiled back an appreciative thank you before turning her attention to Mossop. 'Are you OK?' she asked.

Mossop shook his head and blinked his eyes a couple of times. He clenched and unclenched his right fist and shook his arm, which was aching. 'Yeah, I think so,' he responded. 'Thanks, Stelvina.'

Stelvina touched his shoulder. 'Hey, no problem. That's what I'm here for,' she said gently. 'So, what was all that about?'

'I just wanted to see what would happen if I didn't let go but I don't remember anything after I touched her.'

'Are you some kind of weirdo?' Stelvina joked.

'You were in serious pain but you kept touching her. The light was travelling up your arm towards your face. It's like it was attacking your whole body, like it was taking you over!'

Mossop looked alarmed. 'I didn't know,' he replied. 'I don't remember anything. I guess you saved me.'

Stelvina blushed and glanced down at the floor before looking back up and saying, 'I'm sure you'd do the same for me, Quagoid…' Mossop smiled, not feeling the need to answer that particular question.

Eddie had been quietly thinking whilst Mossop and Stelvina bonded. 'I think it's a defence mechanism,' he said finally, breaking the awkward silence. 'Actually, I think it's defensive and attacking at the same time.' It made sense. An impenetrable defence shield that would immediately spread to anyone who tried to unlock it.

Stelvina nodded in agreement. 'I think you're right, Eddie,' she said.

Mossop's arm was still tingling from the attack but his investigator's senses were beginning to return. 'We need to defrost these guys,' he said, still shaking his arm. 'They are the key to finding out what happened here.'

Stelvina walked over to the oldest technician. His long grey hair and beard seemed to be floating in the blue light that surrounded him. His face looked sad, as if it had been frozen after being given some terrible news. Stelvina looked up at the figure, who was hovering by the master control station. Unlike the other technicians, his eyes were open. Even behind the shimmering blue haze, his eyes looked lifeless. And yet, they seemed to be speaking to her.

Eddie and Mossop walked over and stood either side of Stelvina. 'What's his story?' Eddie asked. 'Why are his eyes open?'

Stelvina looked to her left and refocused onto Eddie's eyes. 'This is the Chief Engineer,' she replied.

Eddie nodded. 'Then we start with him. Mossop…'

Mossop was still looking up at the Chief Engineer. 'Yeah…' he mumbled to himself.

Eddie continued. 'Contact Ramad. Tell him what we've seen here, and find out whether he has anything new for us. Stelvina, I think it's time we had a chat with the king!'

CHAPTER 10

'Papa would be very proud of us.'

The power-bike skidded to a halt in a cloud of dust. Bak Zomak cut the engine and the bike's high-pitched whine stopped abruptly. As the engine stopped, the two stabiliser arms automatically dropped to the floor, creating a leg on either side of the bike. Rok climbed off and walked over to the tangle of vines that covered the rock face in front of the bike. As she busied herself pulling the vines to one side, Bak got off the bike and peered into the distance. He was satisfied that they were alone. 'It's clear,' he said to Rok, reassuringly. Rok nodded and pushed her body weight against the heavy wooden door. As it creaked open, the moon cast just enough light to reveal the passageway behind it. Bak leant across the front of the bike and grabbed the left handlebar. As he did so, he flicked a switch next to the brake lever and, with a gentle whirr, the legs retracted back inside the bike. He then silently rolled it through the door and into the dark tunnel.

Rok pulled a torch from her belt and shone the bright beam down the tunnel. The torch cut a razor-sharp beam of light through the darkness. As the Zomaks came to the end of the tunnel, Rok shone her torch onto the control panel on the wall and waved her hand across the sensor.

The lights revealed the beauty of the foundations. Two hundred years old, they looked as though they had only just been built. Magnificent sand-coloured arches rose up from the floor of the vast cave to its ceiling. Impressive in their own right, they gave no clue as to their purpose. But the Zomaks knew. They knew that above them, King Brude was making the biggest decision of his life.

Bak stabilised the bike and removed the case of gems from the storage compartment. He walked over to the small bank of computer screens, placed the case on the table and looked up at the roof of the cave. Rok joined him at the table, released the lock of the case and opened it, revealing the five green Gems of Dar. 'Do you think he'll go for it?' she asked. Bak wasn't sure. Rok had needed a lot of convincing to steal the gems and she knew now was not the time to be filling her older brother's head with thoughts of failure. She decided not to press him further.

Sensing his sister's concern, Bak placed a hand on one of Rok's shoulders. 'Papa would be very proud of us,' he smiled.

'Do you really think so?' she replied.

Bak nodded. 'We've come home, and we're not going anywhere. We need to get ready. It'll be light soon and Parsus is already dying. It's time for them to hear from us again.'

CHAPTER 11

'Without the Light, everything dies.'

King Brude leant against the stone balcony of his throne room and looked up at the dark sky. Thousands of stars twinkled, as if briefly hiding before revealing themselves to the universe once more.

Brude was the 41st monarch to rule Dar since the Light was first projected onto Parsus. He was in danger of being the last. His huge shoulders heaved as he released a big sigh. He stared up at the shimmering sky, trying to imagine what was happening on Parsus. The increasingly thin atmosphere would already be depriving the planet's surface of its precious protection. The solar winds were already beginning to break through the atmosphere, blowing their fast, increasingly hot breath on everything they touched. The lack of protection from the atmosphere meant that the planet's surface temperature was rapidly rising. As the polar caps melted, the sea level would rise but, within a short period of time, all water would evaporate due to the high temperature. In place of the vast oceans, huge, cavernous valleys would appear, exposing the barren sea-bed. Within a matter of hours, the planet would be nothing more than a bare rock. It would be dead.

Brude turned to face the three young space detectives. 'You do understand? Without the Light, everything dies.'

Eddie looked into the eyes of the broken man that towered above him. His eyes were wet, and Eddie knew that as soon as the king blinked, the water would be released. Sure enough, a tear began its journey down Brude's face, disappearing into the great moustache that almost covered his mouth. Eddie searched for the words that would make the king feel better but time was short. They needed information, and they needed it quickly. Stelvina sensed Eddie's struggle and stepped in with some much needed help. 'We know what will happen, Majesty,' she said calmly. 'We're here to help but we need your guidance.' Brude turned his back on Stelvina and Eddie and looked out across the city. Word had already reached him that some of his advisors wanted the spaceports to be closed to incoming traffic. A thousand years of peace and harmony was beginning to disintegrate before his eyes.

'Do they really expect me to leave?' he growled, a sense of the old battling spirit returning.

Eddie responded. 'That's entirely your decision, Majesty,' he said. 'Parsus is dying. It may never be the same again. But we need to find those gems.'

Brude's head dropped briefly, before his big shoulders straightened. As he turned to face Eddie and Stelvina once more, he seemed to have grown to twice his already huge size. 'Yes,' he said sternly. 'What do you want from me?'

Eddie had a plan, but he also had some questions about the past. He'd listened to Mossop's history lesson in the Star Jumper, and he'd watched the Zomaks' ultimatum. But there were gaps in what he understood. The Zomak Family were exiled on the prisoner planet Cabor but he didn't completely understand why. He also wanted to talk about the Chief Technician but he decided to question Brude about the Zomaks first.

'Majesty,' he said, as respectfully as he could. 'We think that Tak Zomak's son and daughter are behind this.' Brude betrayed no emotion. Eddie continued. 'The family were exiled 10 years ago?' It was a question, but he didn't wait for the king to answer. 'In their ultimatum, the Zomaks spoke about, and these are their words, your crimes against their family. Their exile seems to have coincided with the kidnap of your wife.'

Brude was beginning to frown but said nothing. He let the young space detective continue.

'Did you suspect Tak Zomak of having something to do with the disappearance of your wife? I thought she was kidnapped by a Praal warlord?'

Eddie was beginning to get worried. He was challenging the ruler of an entire planet here. It wasn't something that you did every day but he needed answers, urgently. Brude looked deep into Eddie Poncho's questioning eyes. Eddie had been bold and direct. He'd got straight to the point, putting the king on the spot in a way that few people had ever done. How much did Poncho know? It was as though the space detective was looking into his very soul, searching through his past, digging up long buried memories. How much longer could he keep this secret? Perhaps it was time to relive himself of the enormous guilt that he'd felt for so long. His people were in danger and people on Parsus were dying.

As Eddie was beginning to realise, Stelvina always seemed to know what to say at exactly the right time. She finally broke the awkward silence. 'Majesty, Tak was like a brother to you. What did he do?'

The great king's eyes filled with water once again and he plunged his head into his hands. 'He lost my love,' he cried. 'He lost my queen.' Brude's huge shoulders heaved up and down as he began to sob uncontrollably.

Stelvina reached over and placed a hand on the king's shoulder. It briefly startled the king, who looked up into Stelvina's emerald green eyes. 'Was he responsible for your wife's kidnap?' she asked.

The reply was so quiet that they could barely hear it. 'No. But I held him responsible.'

Eddie was getting confused. 'I don't understand,' he said.

Brude seemed broken. He hadn't spoken about that day for 10 years. 'He was supposed to protect us. He lost my queen, what else could I do?'

Eddie was still trying desperately to fill in the

blanks. 'So, he couldn't find the queen after she was kidnapped? And as chief protector of your family... as part of your family, you held him responsible? He was convicted of not doing his duty and you banished his whole family to the prison planet of Cabor?'

Brude looked at the floor of his palace and spoke in a whisper. 'There was no investigation. There was no trial. On my orders, and my orders alone, Tak, his wife and their two young children, Bak and Rok, were taken from their home in the middle of the night. Within a day, their transport had landed on Cabor. They were dropped into the wastelands of the great forest and left. There was no hope for them. If the night creatures hadn't eaten them by first light, they would surely be captured by any one of a hundred warlords. I didn't expect to hear the name Zomak again during my lifetime.'

Eddie and Stelvina looked at each other. Neither could believe what they had just been told. 'There was no investigation or trial?' Eddie asked, again not waiting for an answer. In the space of a few minutes, he'd lost all respect for the king and wasn't too bothered about hiding the fact. 'You condemned your friend and his family? You held them responsible and condemned them to death? Except they didn't die, did they? Well, at least two of them didn't. And now,

10 years later, the Zomaks have returned home. Except they're not young children anymore, are they? Who knows what lives they've led for the last 10 years? Who knows what evil they've suffered? More to the point, who knows how long they've been planning this chaos?'

Brude looked up. The tears were streaming down his face. 'I'm sorry,' he said.

CHAPTER 12

'You have one more day…'

Eddie's interrogation of Brude was brought to an abrupt halt by Mossop's arrival. 'Majesty,' he said, dipping his head in recognition of the king and completely unaware of what Brude had just admitted to his colleagues. 'Commander Ramad's on the line. We've had a new communication from the Zomaks.' And with that, he pressed his communicator and the familiar face of the Chief of the Space Detective Agency appeared in front of them.

'Good Morning, Majesty,' Ramad said, immediately recognising that all was not quite what he was expecting.

'Er, do you have some news for me?' Brude hadn't spoken to Ramad for a while. He assumed that the old detective knew all about his treatment of Tak Zomak but wasn't in the mood to go over it again so soon. He also knew that Eddie would be updating his chief and contented himself with that. 'Hello, Max. I wish I was seeing you under happier circumstances. Your excellent detectives will update you, I'm sure. They say they have a plan. And I gather you have news from the Zomaks. Please, continue.'

Ramad looked at Eddie, who nodded reassuringly in response. Satisfied that Eddie had things under control with Brude, Ramad was happy to proceed. 'Majesty, we've just received this short message. We don't know when it was recorded but they definitely weren't in the Spectral Chamber at the time.' Ramad's face disappeared and was replaced by the large blue 'Z', shortly followed by an image of Bak Zomak.

'Brude, are you watching? Parsus has little more than one day before it returns to the barren, lifeless state that it was in a thousand years ago. For every hour that you sit on your hands, wrestling with your conscience, Parsus descends into a chaos that will take another thousand years to repair.

'Parsians will soon start heading towards Dar, a whole civilisation searching for a new home. Unless, of course, you choose to condemn these innocents to a life in the stars. That's your style, isn't it, Brude? To condemn. To remove life. To punish without explanation.

'You have one more day to inform the people of Dar that you are leaving the planet and passing control to the Children of Zomak. One more thing: if you take this honourable course of action, we expect to hear the reasons too. Darians have the right to know what a coward the Great King really is.

'We are watching…

'We are waiting...'

Bak's face was replaced by Rok, who was juggling three of the gems. As Rok finished juggling, she looked up and grinned. And then her face was replaced by the big, blue 'Z'.

Brude looked on, horrified and full of guilt. The sight of Rok Zomak juggling the Gems of Dar like a cheap entertainer was too much for him. The Zomaks were now taunting him, and every one of their words felt as though a sharp knife was being plunged deep into his heart. Eddie and Stelvina both looked at the king. They now knew exactly what the Zomaks were referring to when they said they wanted him to explain the reasons to his people. Eddie could sense that some of his anger towards Brude was now being replaced by sympathy. What decision could this proud man make? Within hours, millions of people would be dying. Should he continue to protect his past and allow Eddie's planet to die? But what of the Zomaks? If they weren't found, what would they do next? Surely the death of Parsus wouldn't be the end of the job. Wouldn't they continue to terrorise the solar system until they were satisfied that they had their revenge?

Ramad's face had reappeared. 'Eddie, King Brude said you had a plan.'

'Yes, sir. Mossop touched the light that was surrounding all of the technicians in the Spectral Chamber. It's like a parasite. The longer he touched it, the more it attacked him. If Stelvina hadn't pulled his arm away when she did, I think he'd be floating in the chamber right now.'

Ramad stroked his silver beard. 'Interesting,' he said.

Eddie continued. 'We need to find a way to release the technicians, starting with the Chief Engineer. There's something different about the way he looks. We think he might be able to tell us how the Zomaks got in…'

'The gems!' Eddie was interrupted by Brude. The three detectives all looked at the king.

'What about them, Majesty?' Stelvina responded.

For the first time since the space detectives arrived, the briefest of smiles flickered across the king's face. 'Sardon, the Chief Engineer…' he said. 'Stelvina, the gems give life. You of all people know this. Once a gem is placed in the Spectral Chamber, you can redirect the Light and point it at Sardon. It will release him. He's worked in the Chamber for over 20 years. He knew Tak. Release him. I'm sure he is the answer that we're all looking for.'

'That's a great plan, Majesty,' said Stelvina, slightly disrespectfully. 'But where do we find a gem? I mean, if there were spare gems lying around, we could just start the Light again!'

Brude smiled. 'Stelvina,' he said softly, 'you will find what you're looking for in your own village.' Stelvina frowned, confused by the king's words.

Brude smiled gently. 'There is a sixth gem,' he said.

Stelvina's eyes widened in disbelief. 'A sixth gem. What do you mean?' she demanded.

Ramad interrupted. 'I'm not sure I understand this either, Majesty,' he said.

A sudden sense of hope filled Brude's whole body, as if someone had suddenly handed him the key to his freedom. 'A little security that was put in place when the Darian Light was built a thousand years ago. A sixth gem was crafted and has been cared for by a very special family ever since.'

The throne room fell silent.

Brude walked towards Stelvina and placed a hand on each of her shoulders. 'I believe you know the person that protects it on behalf of our people,' he whispered. 'Do you think it's a coincidence that you are here? You *are* the gems.' Stelvina's mouth opened and her eyes widened. Her heart was beating so hard that it was like a drum being bashed inside her head. King Brude allowed himself another smile. 'Stelvina,' he said, 'the sixth gem is being looked after by your own father. In many ways, he, no, *your* family are the guardians of the Darian Light. Go to your father. Collect the sixth gem and we can save Parsus.'

Stelvina was rapidly falling into a state of shock. She looked at Eddie and Mossop but neither really knew what to say. After a few seconds, Eddie turned to Ramad's flickering face and said, 'It's a plan, sir.'

Ramad agreed and stroking his beard replied, 'It's

the plan. OK, Majesty, can you provide a team of the Royal Guard to accompany Stelvina to Mount Sukat?'

'Of course. They're at your disposal, Commander Ramad.'

'Thank you,' Ramad replied. 'Stelvina, I know this is a shock but we don't have much time left. Are you up to this?'

Stelvina had a thousand questions that she wanted the answer to but she knew that this wasn't the time. Her duty came first and the future of two planets relied on finding the missing gems. She stiffened her body, which immediately made her taller, and replied firmly, 'Yes, sir.'

'Good. Majesty,' Ramad said sternly, turning his face to the king. 'Is there anything more that can help us?'

Brude thought for a couple of seconds before replying, 'Have you tried the Zomaks' old house? It's on the edge of the city, near the coast. It's been empty since…' Brude's voice trailed off. He knew that he bore responsibility for the Zomaks' terrible act of vengeance but he didn't want to upset the sense of co-operation that was now the priority.

Ramad stroked his silver beard again and gave Brude a slightly suspicious look. But like the king, he knew that now was a time for positive action, not picking over the bones of the past. He nodded. 'OK. Eddie, Mossop: take a trip to the Zomaks' house. It's a long shot but they might be there or at the very least might have paid it a visit, for old time's sake. I'm sure the king can arrange for you to be sent the co-ordinates.' Then the old detective looked at King Brude. 'Majesty, whatever happened in the past, right now it's about recovering those gems. We're going to need all the resources you can offer to make that happen.'

It wasn't a request, and Brude knew it. 'Of course, Commander,' he said, bowing his head in respect as he spoke.

'Thank you,' Ramad responded. 'Space Detectives: Major Shim will contact you for a progress report.' Ramad's face vanished as quickly as it had appeared, and with that, Eddie and Mossop nodded to the king and made their way back to the Star Jumper to collect their power-bikes.

Brude turned to Stelvina. 'I know this isn't easy for you, Stelvina.'

What a ridiculous thing to say, she thought, of course it wasn't, but before she could reply Brude said reassuringly, 'Go to your father. Collect the gem. Bring it and your father back here. We don't have much time. Now, are you ready to be a hero?' he asked.

Stelvina took a deep breathed and smiled. 'Yes. I am!'

CHAPTER 13

'Does it hurt?'

'I'll see you at the ship,' Mossop said to Eddie as they left the gleaming white archway of the Royal Palace.

Eddie looked quizzically at his old friend. 'What are you on about?' he fired back.

Mossop gestured towards Stelvina, who had left before them. She was now standing alone at the entrance to the Royal Garden. 'I'm just going to check that she's alright,' he explained, slightly defensively.

Eddie raised his eyebrows and smiled. 'Ah, the old Mossop charm. How could she possibly resist?' he replied, sarcastically. Mossop nudged his shoulder into Eddie's as they walked, which made Eddie stumble. Eddie held his hands up in mock apology and said, 'I guess I asked for that, Mossop.' He gently slapped a hand on Mossop's back. 'Seriously, this is a big deal for her. Make sure she's OK, I'll see you on the flight deck. But don't be too long,' he teased, pointing a finger at his old friend.

As Eddie walked past Stelvina he wished her luck before disappearing down the underground walkway to Dar's central spaceport.

Mossop stopped at the entrance and smiled at Stelvina. She looked particularly alone, lost in any one of a thousand thoughts that she must have been having. She looked up from the ground and out across the beautiful gardens in front of her. Without looking at Mossop she said, 'What was all that about?'

Mossop hadn't realised that she'd seen he and Eddie talking. 'I just told Eddie that we have to make sure you're OK,' he replied. 'Why don't we sit down for five minutes?' he suggested, gesturing towards a beautifully carved stone bench that sat under a giant froo tree.

Stelvina smiled gently. 'Do you have time?' she asked. Mossop nodded and smiled. Feeling slightly embarrassed, Stelvina smiled back at him. 'Thank you,

Quagoid. That's very kind,' she replied.

When they reached the bench, Stelvina sat down. The bench was so big that it made her look half as tall. Mossop looked up at the tall tree and breathed in as deeply as he could. 'Ah, there's nothing like the smell of froo zest to clear your head, is there?' he said light-heartedly as he sat down next to Stelvina. 'So, that was a bit intense in there. How are you feeling?'

Stelvina looked down at her hands, which were tightly clamped against one another. 'I don't know really,' she said quietly. She hadn't even begun to start working that one out. 'It's a shock, you know? I haven't been home for six months. Actually, I haven't really had much contact with Papa at all recently. And all of a sudden, my family are a major part of this mission. It's like our lives have been turned upside down by the gems being stolen. And my family have been hiding this sixth gem that might be the saviour of two planets and I didn't even know about it. I really don't know what I'm going to say to him when I see him.'

Mossop blinked his eyes from side to side, as he always did when something important was said or had just happened. 'You're in a very difficult situation, aren't you?' he replied thoughtfully. 'I guess your dad will explain everything.' He paused briefly whilst he worked out what he was going to say next. 'Don't be too hard on him,' he continued hesitantly. He didn't want to upset her but felt the need to say something reassuring. 'Secrets are our life, Stelvina. You know that. The safest way to protect the sixth gem was for as few people as possible to know about its existence.'

Stelvina looked into Mossop's large black eyes. Of course, he was right, she knew that. It just seemed like such a big secret. 'I know. I'll work it out when I see him,' she replied.

Mossop looked across the garden and up at the twinkling tower that housed the Spectral Chamber. He tried to imagine what it looked like with the Darian Light shooting out the top of it as it began its life-giving journey through the stars. Stelvina seemed to instinctively know what he was thinking and answered the question for him. 'It looks beautiful, and all the more so because you know what it's doing,' she said.

Mossop smiled and nodded in agreement. 'Yeah, I bet it does. I look forward to seeing it.' He patted his hands on his knees and stood up. 'I better get going. Eddie will be going into one,' he said, still smiling.

There was silence for a few seconds whilst Stelvina decided whether she was going to ask what she wanted to ask. She decided not to but then, for some reason, blurted out, 'Does it hurt?'

Mossop frowned and a look of complete confusion fell across his face. That was a bit random, he thought. 'Does what hurt?'

'When you Trace. Does it hurt you?'

Mossop's confusion immediately turned to surprise at Stelvina's unexpected question. As he sat back down on the stone bench, his shoulders dropped and he looked at the ground. Stelvina felt an immediate and massive sense of guilt. She immediately regretted asking the Quagoid. 'Mossop, I'm so sorry. I didn't mean…'

But before she could finish the words, Mossop raised his head and placed a hand on her arm. 'It's OK,' he said reassuringly. He looked down again before adding quietly, 'To be honest, I don't know.'

Now it was Stelvina's turn to look confused. 'You mean you don't remember?' she asked.

Mossop laughed and looked back up at his fellow detective. 'No, I mean actually don't know. I've never done it.' Stelvina definitely felt guilty now. How could she have been so stupid as to assume that he had? She grabbed his hand and gave it a gentle squeeze. Mossop smiled in appreciation of her gesture.

'It's funny,' he continued, 'I've heard about it. I've been told how it will feel by older Quagoids that have done it. They say that it hurts like hell but they can't say for how long. It depends on what you've protected the other person from. It could be for a few seconds or it could be for hours.' He paused. 'It could even be for days. They say it's the most intense pain you can imagine, but not to worry about that because when the time comes, if you're going to do it you won't even think about it. You'll just do it, you know? I mean, they don't even teach you how to Trace. They say if you do it, it'll be because you instinctively know that it's the right thing to do. It's something about our genetic make-up. When the time comes, you'll just follow your instinct. You'll either do it or you won't, and if you do, you won't think about the pain. You'll just know that saving that person's life is the right thing to do.'

Mossop paused and locked his black eyes onto Stelvina's emerald green ones. 'I guess at some point you will think about the 10 years of your own life that you've lost,' he said thoughtfully.

Stelvina sat in silence, dumb-struck by what she was hearing. She wanted to say something but couldn't think of anything useful to say. Mossop took a deep breath and continued.

'You are basically taking that person back in time to when they were last safe and placing them back there. But a successful Trace depends on what state they are in when you begin. If they've stopped breathing, you'll only have a few minutes to trace their timeline back before their brain stops functioning. If they die during the Trace, you also die.' Stelvina sat in stunned silence.

'Apparently, it can take a while to fully recover afterwards but it depends on the individual.' Mossop was almost whispering now. 'Some recover almost immediately, others take weeks and get pretty sick. I guess you just hope that you're never in that situation, although it's considered an honour if you are. And if you choose to save someone's life, well…' He paused. 'It's kind of a major sacrifice for the good of someone else, you know?'

Stelvina shook her head slowly. She thought back to the way she'd greeted Mossop and Eddie on their arrival and felt ashamed. She was trying to impress, but now she just felt like a prize wazoon. 'About what I said on the flight deck…' she stuttered.

Mossop laughed. 'Actually, I quite enjoyed it,' he replied. He looked up again at the Spectral Chamber. It was time to go.

Stelvina smiled gently and nodded. 'I feel better, Mossop. I won't forget this conversation. Thank you,' she said, pulling the hood of her white cloak over her head to protect her from the chill air. 'As I said, let's hope that we don't have to use these gifts on this mission.' And with a swish of her cloak, she turned away from Mossop and walked off to join her escort.

As Mossop watched Stelvina disappear from view he smiled to himself. 'I don't think we're going to be that lucky...'

CHAPTER 14

'Let's get the hell out of here.'

Commander Max Ramad turned to the bank of screens in front of him. His eyes darted from one terrible scene to another: from the chaos of the desperate mass of humanity at the entrance to the spaceport, to the fires that were engulfing the great forest, to the mid-air collisions as the thousands of unauthorised spacecraft filled the air. Time was running out. His home planet was dying before his very eyes, and its only hope of survival lay with three young space detectives' ability to find five green stones.

Ramad stood up and looked around the room. The Command Centre was full of dedicated young people: their heads down, getting on with the latest mission… saving a planet or two. Even by the standards of the SDA, this was not an ordinary day. There they were, as committed and focussed on the job as ever. He was so proud of them. But Ramad knew that deep down, each and every one of them was asking themselves the same question that he was asking himself. When are *we* getting out of here?

There were less than 24 hours left before Zero Day. The mission had to continue, even if Zero Day was reached. He had a responsibility to these people. They all looked up to him. They all looked to him for leadership. And the Space Detective Agency had to survive.

As he looked around, Ramad's eyes met those of his deputy, Major Shim. They both knew what the other was thinking. Shim stood up and walked into the screened area where the commander's work station was. 'Sir?' Shim asked, not really asking a question.

Ramad placed one of his large hands on Shim's shoulder. This was a very sad moment in his life but he couldn't wait much longer. 'It's time for me to make the announcement, Annete,' he said, holding back the emotion he felt inside.

Shim nodded calmly. 'Yes sir. The transporter is ready. Once the security protocols have been completed, we can board and take off. The families are already in orbit, awaiting orders for a destination.' Shim spoke with confidence, knowing that she'd organised the safe evacuation of her colleagues and their loved ones. She was a professional and she had a job to do, but that didn't mean that she wasn't hurting inside. After graduating from the academy, she'd moved her mother to Parsus and made it their home. Her mother was old and sick now, and Shim knew that she would struggle to cope with starting a new life in space. She had no idea whether she'd even see her again. Everyone in the room, everyone in the Space Detective Agency, was in exactly the same situation. Some of her colleagues were young, their mothers and fathers were quite young, some had brothers and sisters. She could see the worry in their eyes and was hurting for them. But she was also very proud of their courage and professionalism. In a time of crisis, they were completely dedicated.

Shim looked into the eyes of her mentor. She knew that he had his own feelings to deal with. Parsus was her adopted home but he was born here. She took a breath and tried to sound reassuring. 'It's the right time, Max,' she said.

Ramad smiled. 'Thank you, Annette. After I've made the announcement, contact Stelvina and find out how far she is from Mount Sukat. We need that gem.'

'Of course, sir,' she replied. 'Eddie and Mossop are going to check in once they've scoped out the Zomaks' old house. Ramad nodded, turned back to his desk and jabbed his finger at the communications panel. As he walked away from his desk, a short, two-toned sound filled the air, prompting everyone in the room to stop what they were doing and look towards their commanding officer. Ramad stood in front of his operations team and took a deep breath.

'Ladies and gentlemen,' Ramad began, 'the time has come…' He paused, catching the slight choking in his throat. He took a second to compose himself before continuing. 'The time has come to leave our home. Time is short and precious, so I'm not going to say much now. You all knew that this moment would arrive. Your families are safe but, of course, I cannot say when you will see them again. I know you would not expect me to. At the moment, our priority is to find the missing gems and restore the Darian Light. Our agents on the ground are chasing leads and we hope to have information on the location of the Zomaks within the next couple of hours.'

Ramad paused again and took a deep breath.

'I know it feels like we're running away, it certainly feels like that to me. But the Space Detective Agency must and will survive. And whether we find the gems or not, the Zomaks must be found. I'm very proud of you all. Now let's start protecting our data. Shut everything down… and let's get the hell out of here.'

CHAPTER 15

'Home!'

Shim walked back to her station and picked up the photograph of her mother. She removed it from its case and placed it safely in one of the pockets on the inside of her jacket. She zipped the jacket up and patted it where the photograph was. Then she sat down and touched the communications screen in front of her. The screen lit up and she pressed the word 'Emerald', Stelvina's code name. 'Base to Emerald. Base to Emerald. Silver here. Report E.T.A. Mount Sukat.'

The sound of wind-rush filled Shim's ear, which

told her that Stelvina was still on the road. As soon as she heard the Major's voice, Stelvina punched a button on her steering wheel and, as if by magic, the windscreen extended above and behind her head, creating a sealed roof. Now that she could hear Shim properly, Stelvina responded. 'Hello Major. My E.T.A. is 10 minutes. How are things there?'

Even though the Command Centre was beginning to resemble an ants' nest, Shim replied calmly. 'The planet's dying quickly, Stelvina. We've just started the security protocols in preparation for evacuating headquarters. It's life in space for us until this mission is over and even then, it probably won't be possible to return to Parsus. Even if you find the gems before Zero Day, it'll still be years before Parsus becomes stable again.'

Stelvina knew that the SDA needed to take the decision to evacuate sooner rather than later. She'd never even visited Parsus, let alone been to headquarters. It looked like she wouldn't be going anytime soon. 'Where will we go?' she asked.

'I really don't know,' came the reply. 'It's something we'll have to look at very carefully when this job is over, and we have to think about the families, of course.'

Stelvina knew that Shim would be worried about her mother. She was on her way to see her own father for the first time in months and understood the feelings of being separated from your only parent. 'Your mama's safe, then?' she asked with concern in her voice.

'Yes, thank you, Stelvina. She's safely on board the transport with the rest of the families. Now listen, do you remember what I told you?'

Stelvina thought for a second. She'd had many conversations with the Major during her time training at the SDA Academy on Zota. Shim had never been short of a few words of encouragement or some good advice. But now, as she was heading home to meet her father, the 'Protector of the Secret Gem', she knew exactly what Shim was talking about. 'Yes, Major, I do,' she replied. 'You told me that one day, I would be tested beyond what I thought I could handle. That I'd think I wouldn't be able to succeed but that I'm stronger than I think I am, and that everything would be OK.'

Like all good mentors, Shim had a way of helping her protégé find the answers for herself, even if she hadn't asked a question. Shim knew Stelvina well enough to know that she was scared about what the next few hours held in store. She wanted to reassure her. 'This is one of those times, isn't it?' Stelvina continued.

'Yes, it is,' Shim replied. 'You can handle it. Don't think about the bigger picture. Take it one step at a time and you'll get there.'

Stelvina was grateful for the advice and the confidence that Shim had in her but before she could reply, Shim spoke again. 'Oh, and one more thing. I know you have a lot of questions for your father but we don't have much time. We have to get that gem back to the Spectral Chamber.'

Stelvina knew what Shim meant. 'I understand, Major. King Brude said that Papa knows how to install the gem and how to direct its light towards the Chief Engineer. Don't worry, I'll bring him back with me. I'm guessing that if I turn up unannounced asking for the secret gem, he'll know how urgent it is.'

Shim laughed. 'OK, I'm not far away,' she continued. 'I'll report in when we're on our way back to the city.'

'Roger, Emerald. Good luck. Silver out.'

Stelvina cut the transmission and looked ahead at the high mountains that now filled the horizon. Her cruiser swept around a sharp bend and began the long climb up Mount Sukat, its escort of two Darian Royal Guard assault cruisers following a few metres behind.

Stelvina smiled to herself: 'Home!'

CHAPTER 16

'They've been here.'

The two power-bikes came to a sudden stop at the un-gated entrance of the Zomaks' house. In one swift movement, Eddie and Mossop cut their engines, leapt from their bikes and walked into the dark courtyard. Dawn was approaching and the reflection of the rising sun was bouncing off the sea. It provided some light but it wasn't enough to see properly. Mossop walked back to the bikes and turned their headlights on. The entire courtyard and the front of the house lit up.

It didn't take Eddie long to spot the deep, wide tyre tracks that led in and out of the courtyard.

Mossop joined Eddie and knelt down beside the tracks. He brushed his gloved hand over the sharp edge of one of the tracks and watched it merge into the smooth dusty ground. 'Look pretty fresh, don't they?' he said. As Mossop stood up, Eddie nodded. The two young space detectives looked around the courtyard. They both walked back a few steps so that they could get a better view of the tracks. In places, the two lines of tracks criss-crossed over each other, but they both led to and from the play area on the right of the house. Eddie and Mossop walked through the entrance and into the walled courtyard, stopping at the climbing wall.

As they looked around the dusty courtyard, it wasn't hard to see the lines of footprints. Some led to the entrance of the house, some to a small grouping of rocks over to the left, and some back to the climbing wall. 'They've been here,' Eddie said.

'Yeah,' Mossop responded, 'and judging by the crispness of the tracks, not that long ago either.' Mossop lifted his head up and looked towards the sea. He blinked as the breeze hit his face. 'The tide is starting to come in. These tracks will be gone in an hour.'

Eddie followed a set of prints over to the rocks on

the opposite side of the courtyard. He tried to imagine the Zomaks standing here, discussing their handiwork. 'Why here?' he wondered out loud. He pulled his torch from the holder on his belt and turned it on. The powerful beam of white light threw a perfect circle onto the dusty ground at his feet. He flicked the beam around and onto the rocks. Nothing. No prints, other than the ones that led back to the climbing wall, and no signs that the earth around the rocks had been disturbed.

Mossop walked over to the rocks. 'Maybe they were just chatting about their childhood,' he said, placing his right hand on the stone in front of him.

Eddie was confused. 'Maybe…' he agreed.

Mossop removed his own torch, spun around and shone it in the direction of open doorway of the Zomaks' old house. 'We should take a look inside,' he suggested.

The space detectives walked over to the front of the house, stopping at the front door where the footprints ended. They shone their torches at the final prints, which, confusingly, were about two strides from the front door. It seemed obvious that whoever left the prints would have entered the house but the footsteps just ended. There was a dark hole where the front door used to be and Eddie and Mossop now walked over to it. As they shone their torches into the house, they revealed its dusty interior. Both the floors of the doorway and the hall inside were covered in a thick layer of sand, but there were no footprints. 'Maybe they've got wings!' Mossop joked.

Eddie laughed. He turned around and shone the beam of his torch back to the tyre tracks. He was trying to work things out in his mind but this was all beginning to feel like a wild-goose chase. Finally he said, 'You know, I don't think they went inside. I think they just came here for old time's sake. Probably congratulated themselves on a job well done before heading back to the city.'

Mossop agreed, it was the only explanation, although he wondered why they would take the risk. They had to think that the Darian security services would check the house out. 'Yeah,' he replied, 'or to wherever they're actually holed up. I can't believe they've hidden the gems here. They'd want to keep them close, surely? Still, coming here was a bit cocky. Maybe that was part of the plan, to waste our time.'

Eddie was annoyed that they were no closer to finding the Zomaks. Mossop knew his friend well enough to know that he was frustrated and had to feel like they were making progress. 'We should still take a look inside the house,' he said, trying to sound positive.

Eddie nodded. 'You're right, Mossop. We might find something useful. I'll report in first. Why don't you take another look around the courtyard?'

Mossop walked back to the rocks and started to look behind them and at the nearby wall. Eddie shook his head in another act of frustration before flicking the communicator in his ear. 'Fire to base. Reporting.' Major Shim's voice filled his head.

'Base here, Fire. What's the situation down there?'

Eddie frowned. 'We're pretty sure they've been here in the last couple of hours, Major,' he reported to Shim. 'The tracks seem pretty fresh but there's no obvious sign that they went into the house.' As Eddie spoke, the wind was beginning to increase. A tell-tale sign that the tide was coming in. He watched carefully as a misty layer of sand began its journey across the ground in front of him. As it did so, the sharp edges of the tracks were already beginning to soften. This was his confirmation that the Zomaks had not entered the house, at least not during this visit. 'Mossop's having a final look around the courtyard before we enter the house,' he continued.

'OK, Eddie,' Shim replied. 'Be careful. I think we're clutching at straws but you might find something we can use. Stelvina is at Mount Sukat and will be back at the Royal Palace in an hour. Check the house and then get back to the city. Unless you find something in there, call me when you're back at the Spectral Chamber. I want you all there when the Chief comes out of his trance.'

'You mean *if* he comes out!' Eddie responded.

'Well, yes, if,' said Shim. 'That sixth gem is beginning to feel like our one and only chance of finding the Zomaks. OK, Eddie. We're about to board the evacuation transport.'

'Good luck, Major. Out!' Eddie walked over to the rocks and joined Mossop. 'Anything?' he enquired.

Mossop shook his head. 'No, nothing. No tracks, nothing.'

'Mmm, that's what I told Shim. She wants us back at the Spectral Chamber for when Stelvina returns with the gem,' Eddie reported.

'Right, let's get this search done and head back.'

CHAPTER 17

'I've seen that before.'

As the space detectives entered the inner chamber of the house, they immediately put a hand over their mouths and noses. The air was stale and thick, and it made them both cough as soon as it hit the back of their throats. Outside, the sun was slowly rising, but it was still very dark inside the house. The torch beams flickered around the room, mixing with the dusty air and revealing mysterious shapes. Sometimes, part of a piece of furniture would appear or part of an archway that led to another room or a pile of rubbish. 'It stinks in here,' Eddie mumbled from behind his hand.

The inside was a complete wreck. It looked like the whole house had been picked up by a giant hand and shaken a couple of times before being slammed back down on the ground. It was difficult to move around without walking into or treading on something. Eddie carefully worked his way over to the right side of the room and walked through the archway. He aimed his torch at the walls and ceiling. It didn't take him long to work out that he was standing in the kitchen area. Mossop broke the silence. 'I'm going to take a look upstairs,' he said.

Eddie's response was short; something had caught his eye. 'OK, take it easy up there.'

As Mossop's boots clunked up the stone steps behind him, Eddie pointed his torch at the floor and allowed its beam to guide him to the far wall. When he reached the wall, he pointed the beam at the collection of photographs and drawings that were displayed on it. The photographs were of the Zomak family, memories that had somehow survived the 10 years since they'd been dragged from the house by Brude's guards. It looked like the house had been trashed over and over again since that day. Did the Darian security services do it when they turned up to arrest Tak Zomak? Maybe people had lived in the abandoned house over the course of the 10 years.

There was no front door so anybody could get in, although there were no other houses nearby. Eddie wondered why the Zomaks had not taken these precious memories with them to the prisoner planet. Surely they would have wanted them on Cabor? It made Eddie think that the Zomaks probably didn't know they were about to be arrested and sent into exile on another planet. He imagined the security services arriving unannounced. The two young children would have been extremely scared. In fact, they were probably so young that they could have had no understanding of what was happening to them.

Eddie tried to put himself in the same situation, and he didn't like the way it made him feel. He thought back to the things that King Brude had said and he began to feel angry again. Nothing could justify the action that the Zomaks had taken, which might kill millions of innocent people. But he was beginning to understand why they felt so angry and bitter about the way their family had been treated… and by someone who was supposed to be a friend.

Amongst the photographs and drawings was one that particularly grabbed his attention. He stood in front of the colourful drawing and, with his right hand above his shoulder, focussed the torch beam on it. Two children playing with a ball in what looked like an underground cave. Nothing unusual about that, but that background. Huge carved arches that rose up from the floor of the cave before slowly disappearing into the ceiling above. Eddie studied the picture carefully. It had the look of a picture that was drawn by a young child, but one with a lot of talent. He was super impressed with the detail of the drawing and knew that his old friend would be equally impressed: Mossop was also a talented artist.

Eddie's train of thought was interrupted by the sound of Mossop's bootsteps echoing on the stone steps as he walked back down the stairs. Eddie span around and pointed his torch at the steps so that his friend could see more clearly. 'There's nothing of interest upstairs either,' Mossop said. 'Just more heaps of furniture and rubbish,' he added, as he carefully negotiated the final step.

'Come and have a look at this,' Eddie commanded, turning his torch back to the drawing on the wall.

Mossop made his way over to the kitchen to where Eddie was standing. His eyes widened as soon as he saw the drawing. 'I've seen that before,' he said. Eddie frowned. 'In the Zomaks' second message,' Mossop continued, jabbing his finger at the drawing. 'They played here as kids. And now, it's where they're hiding. I'm sure of it.'

Mossop ripped the drawing from the wall. 'Right, let's get back to the palace,' he said, 'I'm sure someone knows where this is. An underground cave with huge sculpted arches. How much of a secret can that be?'

Eddie agreed. 'Let's get out of here. I'll report to Shim once we're on the road.'

CHAPTER 18

'Is it true, Papa?'

The tall captain walked over to the wooden steps and stood next to Stelvina. She looked tiny next to him and even in the half-light of dusk, her white hooded cloak and dress were a big contrast to his mainly red uniform. Stelvina stood at the bottom of the stairs looking up at the front door of the stone cabin, her childhood home. She was trying desperately to find the courage to walk up them. 'He'll be glad to see you, Stelvina,' Captain Orval said, trying to sound reassuring.

'I know,' Stelvina replied quietly. She took a breath, to calm herself down. 'It's just that it's been a while, you know?' She was grateful for her escort's encouragement and took another long, slow, deep breath. As she did so, she allowed the crisp morning mountain air to clear her head. Then she glanced at the captain and said, 'OK, here I go.'

Orval smiled as he watched her walk slowly up the steps towards the big front door. 'We'll be ready to go as soon as you have the gem,' he said to Stelvina's back.

Stelvina stopped before she got to the last step and removed the floppy hood from her head. She turned the upper half of her body and with half a smile said, 'Thank you, Captain Orval.'

Stelvina climbed the last step and slowly reached a hand out towards the large knocker in the middle of the door. She paused for a moment, then grabbed the knocker and gave the door two loud bangs.

She could feel her chest heaving as she waited for the door to open. *This is crazy,* she thought to herself. *It's just Papa. But he's been secretly looking after a sixth Gem of Dar for who knows how long. What other secrets does he have?* Then she said out loud, 'But he doesn't know half of what I get up to!' In an attempt at calming her nerves, Stelvina took another deep breath. As she slowly exhaled, she was interrupted by the sound of the door's lock being turned. She held her breath and watched the door slowly creak open. As it did so, two pairs of emerald green eyes met for the first time in months.

Trufo stood frozen to the spot, a look of disbelief in his eyes. Stelvina found her courage and spoke first. 'Hello, Papa,' she said as confidently as she could. 'I've missed you.'

Trufo's eyes began to shine as the tears gathered on the bottom of his eyelids. As the weight of the water grew, he blinked and two rivers ran down his cheeks. He held both of his large, rough hands out and said, 'My child.' Stelvina fell into her father's arms and buried her head in his chest. As she sobbed, he placed a comforting hand on her head and gently stroked her long white hair. As he did so, he noticed the tall red figure at the bottom of the stairs. Then he looked behind Captain Orval and saw the menacing-looking black assault cruisers, with the Darian Royal Guard insignia clearly visible on their sides. He instantly knew that this wasn't a social visit.

'My child?' he asked.

'Is it true, Papa?' Trufo held his breath. Stelvina asked him once more. 'Papa, is it true? Do you have a sixth gem?'

Trufo looked back down at the captain, who nodded his head as a mark of respect. Stelvina looked back as Orval raised his head, his eyes meeting hers. 'We don't have much time, Stelvina,' he said in a firm but gentle voice.

Stelvina turned back to her father and was about to speak but he got there first. 'I think we should go inside,' he said. 'I'm guessing that if you're here unannounced, and the good captain and his Royal Guard are with you…' Trufo paused, 'then time is precious, eh Captain?' Orval gently nodded his head once more. Trufo smiled. 'Then we'll be as quick as we can, Captain.'

Orval smiled back and replied with a firm, 'Thank you, sir.'

Trufo took his only child's hand and gently guided her into the cabin.

As the heavy door clicked shut behind them, Trufo ushered Stelvina into the warmth of the cabin. Like generations of his family before him, Trufo had lived on Mount Sukat his whole life. His skin was tanned from long days spent in the sun at high altitude, but it still looked very healthy. He didn't have that craggy, weather-beaten skin that can make mountain people look much older than their years.

And his eyes were a clear and bright, white and emerald green, fresh from the cool, crisp mountain air. He was an honest, hard-working man who was proud of his roots on Sukat. But he was especially proud of the part that his ancestors had played in the life of his planet, and that of its neighbour in the stars. His biggest regret was that he could not share his pride with those closest to him. His secret was both his biggest honour, and his biggest curse. And then, this morning, without warning, his space detective daughter appears with an armed Darian Royal Guard escort.

Trufo smiled at Stelvina, who was busy reacquainting herself with the cabin. 'It's good to see you, my child. You must have many questions.' Stelvina nodded, unable to recall a single one of the hundred or so questions that she'd thought of during her journey from the city. Trufo could sense his daughter's anxiety. He decided to take control of the situation. 'Come with me,' he said. 'I'll take you to the gem.'

Stelvina swallowed hard. She'd barely accepted that her father was the protector of the sixth gem. They'd not even spoken about it and now she was about to see it for herself. *Get a grip,* she told herself. *You've got a job to do here.* She pushed her shoulders back and announced confidently, 'You're going to have to come back to the city with me, Papa. We need you to install the gem. I'm told that's something that you can do?'

Trufo smiled at the sudden change in Stelvina's personality. She was a professional now, with a serious job to do. In fact, if she was here for the gem, probably a life-threatening job. He wanted to tell her how proud he was of her but that would have to wait for another time. 'Yes, Stelvina,' he replied, 'I can install the gem. I don't know what's happened, but I know that if you're here then it's serious.'

Stelvina was grateful for her father's understanding of the situation. They were both beginning to see each other in a different light. 'Thank you, Papa,' she said. 'I promise I'll tell you everything once we're on our way.'

Trufo nodded in agreement and waved his hand in the direction of the huge stone fireplace that split the downstairs rooms of the cabin. 'Well,' he said, 'you'd better follow me then.'

CHAPTER 19

'They are life. The gems are us, and we are the gems.'

Trufo walked over to the large fireplace in the centre of the cabin. He was about to clean it and collect wood to make a new fire when Stelvina knocked at the door. That job would have to wait now.

Watching her father standing by the fireplace brought back many memories for Stelvina. The fireplace was traditional of those found in the mountains around Sukat. It was open at both sides, which kept the large cabin warm and if you were being really naughty, you could run all the way around it. In her mind's eye, she could see herself sitting on one side of the fire and her father sitting on the other in the adjoining room. They would have fun playing Zap, a game that Trufo had played when he was a child. Each player would try to hide behind the flickering flames and shout, 'Zap!' in their loudest voice whenever they saw the other player's face. It was a game that Stelvina loved to play with her father, especially during the long, cold winters on Mount Sukat. The fire was the very heart of the cabin.

Stelvina's flashback was interrupted by Trufo ringing the old iron bell that hung from the right side of the fireplace. Stelvina looked up from where the flames would normally have been and smiled at the sound of the bell. Another childhood memory. 'I bet you didn't know it did this,' Trufo said, raising his black eyebrows a couple of times as he grabbed the top of the bell and pulled it towards him.

Stelvina's mouth fell open as the great stone fireplace creaked and slowly began to move to the left of the cabin. As it moved, it revealed a black hole that was slightly smaller than the surface area of the base of the fireplace. As the hole became more visible, Stelvina could see the top of a flight of perfectly carved white stone steps that led underneath where the fireplace had just stood. As the fireplace came to a stop against the wall on the far left of the cabin, Stelvina gasped in amazement. 'How long has that been there?' she asked her father.

Trufo smiled. 'Since before you were born,' he replied. 'Now, do you want this gem or are you going to stand there with your mouth open for the rest of the day?'

Trufo began to walk down the white stone steps. As his legs disappeared, the black hole that was swallowing him suddenly lit up with a brilliant white light. Stelvina followed behind him, running her hand over the cold, smooth walls as she walked down the steps. When Trufo got to the bottom, he stopped in front of the chest-height picture of a woman. He held his hand out and stroked her long, white hair. Stelvina reached the bottom of the steps, saw the picture and cried out, 'Mama!'

As she rested a hand on her father's shoulder, he turned his head towards her and their emerald green eyes met once again. 'You look just like her,' he said, tears forming in his eyes once more.

He looked back at the picture and held the palm of his hand over his wife's smiling face. As he did so, Stelvina's mum said, 'Hello, Trufo.'

Stelvina gasped. She hadn't heard her mum's voice

since she died five years ago. She looked at her dad. 'How is that possible?' she asked.

Trufo gently smiled. 'It's a hologram that reads our family's genetic code,' he explained. 'It activates when our eyes meet. There are only two people in the entire universe who can open this,' he said, as he reached out and gently touched his wife's face with his fingertips. As his fingers connected with the hologram, the picture turned bright green before disappearing completely. He pulled his hand back so that Stelvina could see the contents of the small chamber and its hidden secret.

She leant forwards so that she could get a closer look and gasped when she saw the gem. 'It's beautiful,' she said. Stelvina got as close to the gem as the opening of the chamber would allow. The inside of the chamber was a bright, white light and the gem sat on a comfortable bed of soft white fur. Stelvina instantly recognised the fur as being from the Jamox: the shy, flightless bird that lives on the exposed upper slopes of Mount Sukat. She leant closer and closer to the opening of the chamber, until the tip of her nose was almost touching the gem. It glistened in the bright light, having an almost hypnotic effect on her. She was being drawn in by its power. As her eyes began to focus, she noticed the tiny flares of green light that danced on its shiny surface. It was a magical sight. The flares seemed to be dancing to some unheard tune and as they flickered off the gem. They seemed to merge with her emerald green eyes.

Trufo broke the silence. 'They are life,' he said. 'The gems are us, and we are the gems.'

Stelvina pulled her head away from the chamber and breathed out. She had been so mesmerised by the gem's dancing flares that she hadn't realised she'd been holding her breath. Trufo continued. 'The gem is life, and our family is the protector of that life. You, my child, *are* the gems; as was your mama. Do you feel it?'

Stelvina's heart was pumping so hard that she thought it was going to leap out of her chest and join the gem on its cosy bed of Jamox fur. 'I feel something, Papa, but…' She paused, trying to understand exactly what it was that she felt. 'I feel alive.'

Trufo roared with laughter. 'Yes, my child, ALIVE!' he shouted.

Stelvina clutched her chest and screamed out, 'I'M ALIVE!'

As their laughter began to die out, Trufo reached into the chamber, picked up the gem and held it in the palm of his hand. As he did so, the surface of the gem began to fizzle. The green flares increased in number and length, and then, suddenly, the gem jumped up in his palm and disappeared behind a cage of pure plasma. With his other hand, Trufo picked up the plasma cage. It instantly hardened.

Stelvina looked on, eyes wide open.

Trufo wanted to be sure that Stelvina understood the connection that their family had to the Gems of Dar, which had been mined by their ancestors a thousand years ago. He placed the hardened cage on the fourth step and it turned to plasma once more. 'Pick it up,' he instructed Stelvina, who frowned at his suggestion. 'Go on,' he commanded again. 'Pick it up.' Stelvina slowly leant forwards and touched the green, glowing cage. It fizzled and crackled as the immediate area around her fingertips hardened. Scared, she pulled her hand back quickly. Trufo placed a reassuring hand on his daughter's shoulder and said, 'It's OK. Remember, we are the gems.'

Stelvina took a breath and reached out again. She gently picked up the plasma cage, which instantly hardened into an unbreakable protective box. 'That's amazing,' she gasped, holding the box up and turning it around so that she could inspect all sides of it.

Trufo nodded. 'Yes, it is. It's completely protected

now. The plasma replicates our genes. It knows it's us, it trusts us. We can transport it safely now.' The mountain man paused for a second. 'And we are the only ones who can release it.'

Stelvina had allowed herself to lose track of time and she knew that outside, Captain Orval would be getting impatient. She handed the box to her father and said, 'Thank you, Papa. We need to go now. I'll tell you everything on the way.'

As Stelvina opened the cabin's front door, Orval was walking up the steps. He stopped as soon as he saw her. 'I'm sorry, Stelvina, I was beginning to get worried. Are we ready to go?'

Stelvina felt embarrassed and felt the need to apologise. 'I'm sorry to have kept you waiting, Captain. This is my papa, Trufo,' she said, introducing her father as he was closing the door. 'Right now, he's probably the most important man in the Qenos System,' she added.

Orval placed his hand over his heart. 'Then it will be our honour to escort you and your father back to the city,' he said.

CHAPTER 20

'What have we done?'

Rok Zomak sat cross-legged on the dusty ground of the cave. Bak had gone outside to check the entrance to the cave, leaving his younger sister alone with her thoughts. She looked up at the vast stone arches that rose high above her head. Rok was scared, but she didn't want to admit that to her brother. More than a day had passed and still there was no sign of a response from the Royal Family.

It wasn't like Bak had dragged her to Dar to steal the gems. She hated Brude for what he'd done to their family but if she really thought about it, she was too young to remember anything about their life on Dar. She had brief flashbacks of certain images, like the one she was looking at now. She could remember playing under the big stone arches but she couldn't remember how they used to get into the cave, even though Bak had told her lots of times. They'd played in that cave whilst their father worked above them guarding the king, making sure everyone was safe. Every once in a while, either Tak Zomak or his best friend would bring them some food and drink, and then, at the end of the day, their father would take them back to their seaside home at top speed.

It sounded like a great life, but Rok couldn't remember any of it. Except the big stone arches that she was looking up at now. She remembered those.

She uncrossed her legs, stood up and walked over to the bank of screens in the middle of the cave. Her eyes flicked between each of the screens. The first carried a news feed from Parsus. Devastation was beginning to rip through the planet and the landscape was beginning to change drastically. The surface water had almost completely evaporated, and piles of dead sea-creatures laid on what had once been the sea bed. Fuelled by the fierce solar winds and the increasingly thin atmosphere, fires raged through cities and forests, destroying everything in their path. Most of the footage was from airborne craft and judging by the quality of the pictures, the broadcasts wouldn't be lasting for much longer.

Rok's eyes flicked right to the next screen and a static shot high above the spaceport. It was total chaos. A great seething mass of life, all fighting for a place on one of the two giant transport ships, which appeared to be the only remaining spacecraft on the flight deck. 'They're the only two left…' she said out loud.

Below that screen, the Darian News Agency was carrying a feed from Dar's central spaceport. The presenter was talking about how the authorities were now denying all requests to land and were about to close the port. The camera panned away to a shot of the sky behind the presenters head. Hundreds of spacecraft, of various shapes and sizes, were either criss-crossing the early morning sky or were at a complete standstill in mid-air whilst their occupants decided what to do or where to go next. Rok wondered where all these people were going to go. They had made the trip to Dar from Parsus but were now being refused entry. It was unlikely that they'd have enough fuel to get to another planet. She guessed that most would land on Dar unofficially.

The presenter announced that there were calls for

the Darian army to start patrolling the planet's outer sphere and to use force to stop people from entering. 'The people are saying it's time to protect Dar,' Rok heard the presenter say.

Rok's eyes flicked back to the scene from Parsus, just in time to see the mid-air collision of two spacecraft that were trying to escape from the dying planet. She gasped in horror at what she'd just witnessed. For a few seconds, her body froze. She had caused these two ships to crash into one another. She had caused the deaths of everyone on board. How many had she killed? Who were they, what were their names? Were there children on board? How many more people had already died because of her actions? How many more were about to die?

She raised her hands to her mouth as she watched the fireball fall from the sky, leaving a trail of thick, black smoke in its wake. The camera followed the fireball's final journey before it disappeared into a large crater that was once the biggest stretch of landlocked water on Parsus. Up until this moment, Rok had been immune from the reality of her actions. But now, the full horror and consequences of stealing the gems was unfolding in front of her. One planet was dying before her very eyes. The other was trying to save itself by turning its back on a thousand years of history and tradition.

And then, as the sense of guilt completely overcame her, Rok Zomak let out an ear-piercing scream that echoed around the vast underground cave. When the explosion of energy finally came to an end, she slumped forward. Her whole body was shaking uncontrollably. She leant over and grabbed the edge of the table with both hands, tensing her body as she tried desperately to control the shaking. She opened her eyes, which were bright red from the inflamed blood vessels. Just as she thought she'd got some control back over her body, her head and shoulders slumped down and she half-collapsed onto the table.

As Rok buried her head in her hands, Bak Zomak burst through the tunnel and into the cave. 'What the hell was that?' he shouted, running over to the bank of screens that his sister was now slumped in front of. Rok didn't answer: she was so numb from the emotion of what she'd seen that she hadn't even realised Bak was standing next to her. Bak grabbed Rok's shoulder, shook it and tried to get her attention. 'Rok, what's happened? Was that you screaming? I thought someone was here. What the hell's wrong with you?'

The combination of Bak's shaking and yelling slowly brought Rok back into the moment. Almost without Bak noticing, his sister raised her head and looked up at the screens in front of her. 'What have we done?' she whispered between the sobbing.

Bak was confused. 'What do you mean?' he replied.

Rok pointed aggressively at the scenes of carnage that were unfolding in front of them. 'Look,' she yelled, jabbing her finger at each of the screens in turn. 'Look, look, look!' She turned around and looked deep into her brother's eyes. 'What... have... we... done?' she pleaded.

Bak glanced at the screens. 'What do you mean?' he asked, frowning. 'We knew this would happen.'

Rok let go of the table and stood up, her face now level with Bak's. She was still shaking from the raw emotion of what she'd seen but now, she was also angry with her brother for not recognising the tragedy that was on the screens. 'You told me that Brude would leave. You said that he wouldn't let Parsus die, that he wouldn't let Dar be overrun. But he hasn't done anything. We've had no contact, we're stuck in this cave with no escape plan, millions of people are dying and it's all because of us.'

Bak shook his head. 'You're wrong,' he said.

'Brude is a coward. He ruined our family and he knows it. He's got no choice, he has to negotiate.'

'But what about those people?' she yelled into Bak's face.

Bak took a step back and lowered his voice. Rok was having doubts, he could see that. But more than that, she was right on the edge. He knew that he needed to calm her down or she'd be no use. He placed a hand on each of Rok's shoulders and tried to sound reassuring. 'I understand that you're having doubts about what we've done but you have to trust me. When have I ever let you down?' Rok sighed and looked down at the ground. She was confused by his refusal to acknowledge the death that she just witnessed with her own eyes. Bak placed his hands on each side of Rok's face and lifted her head up so that their eyes met once more. 'Brude *will* make a deal. Now, get ready to send another message. I'm going to finish camouflaging the entrance to the cave.'

CHAPTER 21

'You might want to stand over there.'

Not for the first time today, Trufo had tears in his eyes. He walked slowly into the room, scarcely able to believe what he was seeing. As he moved between the floating bodies, he gave each one the same attention as the next. When he got to Alexa Karel, he stopped and looked up at her. He reached out but felt his arm being swiftly yanked back. 'I wouldn't do that, sir,' Mossop warned with a friendly smile. Trufo turned and looked at the grinning Quagoid. 'Personal experience!' Mossop added by way of an explanation.

Stelvina walked over and joined them in front of the floating Alexa. 'Eddie's still at the palace,' she reported.

'What's the hold-up?' demanded Mossop.

Stelvina gave her father a soothing stroke on the shoulder and offered him a reassuring look. 'Brude's getting ready to make an announcement. Eddie's guiding him through it.'

Mossop was concerned. He hadn't sensed much fight in the king and wondered if he was going to cave in to the Zomaks' demands. 'He's not giving up, is he? He can't go to Parsus now,' he said. 'It's dying!'

Stelvina shook her head. 'Don't worry, Mossop. He's going to tell his people that he's not going to abandon them. That whatever happens, he's not giving in.'

Mossop grumbled to himself. *Perhaps the old king does have some fire in his belly after all.*

'Besides,' Stelvina added with a sudden lightness in her voice, 'Prince Tomeke is helping him.' She paused before adding in a very soppy voice, 'We Darians absolutely adore him… obviously.'

Mossop gave Stelvina a long, lingering stare before blinking his eyes. Stelvina smiled gently. She knew that her comment would get to Mossop but her teasing didn't last long as she continued to update him. 'Brude wants to tell the people that we're on the Zomaks' trail but Eddie has told him not to say anything. We don't know what they know about what's happening on Parsus or here. We have to assume that they have access to cameras and broadcasts.'

Mossop stroked the point of his chin. 'Mmm, and what about him?' he asked, nodding towards the Chief Engineer.

'Eddie wants us to get on with it. He'll be here as quickly as he can,' Stelvina replied.

'OK,' said Mossop, taking control. He looked across to Trufo. 'Are you up for this, sir?'

Trufo didn't respond. He was still looking up at Alexa, wondering whether she was remotely aware of what had happened to her.

'Papa,' Stelvina said loudly in an attempt to get his attention. She grabbed his hand, which brought him out of his trance. 'It's time. You *can* do this, can't you?'

Trufo looked at his daughter and nodded. 'Let's go,' he replied firmly.

Trufo walked over to the Spectral Chamber, which was located in the centre of the room. He looked into the now open gem chamber and placed a hand over one of the five holes. Until yesterday, and for the last one thousand years, a bright green life-giving gem had called it home. He looked up at the series of magnifiers, and beyond those to the stellar tracker, which ensured that the Darian Light was permanently directed at Parsus. Stelvina and Mossop joined Trufo at the chamber. Trufo took the plasma box from his bag and placed it gently on the control panel in front of him. 'The first thing we need to do is redirect this magnifier towards him,' he said pointing to the first, and smallest magnifier that was positioned just above the gem chamber. 'Stelvina, can you go to the other side, please, and tell me when you can see Sardon through the magnifier?' Stelvina did as her father asked, moving quickly to the opposite side of the chamber.

Trufo was just about to commence recalibrating the magnifier when Eddie walked in. His focus suddenly broken by the swish of the door, Trufo looked up from the control panel. 'Have I missed anything?' Eddie demanded. Trufo frowned.

Stelvina made the introductions. 'Papa, this is Eddie Poncho: a fellow agent from the SDA. Eddie, this is my father, Trufo. We were just about to begin.'

Eddie was pleased that he'd got to the chamber in time to see the magician at work, but now was not the time for a long introduction. 'Brude's making his announcement,' he said sharply. 'Please, Trufo, continue your work.'

Trufo admired Eddie's focus. He smiled and turned his attention back to the control panel. As his fingers moved towards the key pad, he hesitated for a moment. In the years since his own father had passed the safe-keeping of the sixth gem to him, it had never occurred to him that he would actually have to do this one day. For all of his adult life, he'd looked after the gem. He'd protected it, and now he was about to bring it to life. Would he know what to do? He took a deep breath and closed his eyes for a few seconds as he tried to visualise what he was about to do. Then, he slowly allowed the tips of his fingers to gently rest against the keys.

Without warning and in a blur of activity, his fingers began typing strings of source code into the computer. As the characters of the bright green code lit up the screen in front of him, the magnifier sprang into life. First, the glass moved into a 45-degree angle. Then, its carbonite holder began to rotate towards

Sardon. Stelvina crouched down so that she would be able to see through the magnifier when it reached the correct position. As it slowly progressed on its journey, she held her right arm up. One of the chief's arms came into view.

'Nearly there…'

Then his back, with the mane of long grey hair. 'Almost…'

And then, when the second arm appeared: 'Stop!'

With an extravagant flourish of his right hand, Trufo hit a button on the key pad and the magnifier clicked to an abrupt stop. He walked around to where his daughter was standing, bent down and peered through the magnifier. 'Excellent,' he whispered quietly to Stelvina before returning to the control panel. He punched in some more code and locked the magnifier into its new position.

The three young space detectives stood in silence as they watched Trufo work. He was in the swing of it now, punching in ever-increasing strings of code. Occasionally, he looked up at the screen, subconsciously checking the long green lines, but his fingers kept moving. They were working at a frantic pace as he prepared the chamber to receive the gem. Stelvina looked in wonder at what she was witnessing.

Where had he got all this knowledge from? Was she expected to learn how to do this?

Eddie leant across to Mossop and whispered, 'Look at this. There's no way the Zomaks could have done this without help.' Mossop nodded in agreement and glanced at Sardon's floating body. 'Someone in this room knows something. Let's hope it's the chief or we'll be here until next week interrogating technicians.' Eddie smiled. Mossop's dark humour was always at its sharpest when the chips were down.

Eddie looked back at Trufo just in time to see him stop typing. The mountain man looked up at the screen for one final check. Then he looked through the chamber at Stelvina and said firmly, 'It's time.'

Trufo carefully placed the palms of his hands on either side of the plasma box. As he did so, the box fizzed and crackled. After a few seconds, the hardened box turned to pure plasma. A few seconds more and the plasma began to disappear until, with a final fizz at the intersection of three corners, it disappeared completely.

Mossop gasped. 'How the…?'

Stelvina smiled proudly. 'It knows my family. We protect it. I made that box appear with my own hands, you know.' Eddie and Mossop exchanged glances.

Ramad was right: Stelvina *was* full of surprises.

'It's beautiful,' Eddie said.

Trufo picked up the gem and held it up to the light. His emerald green eyes met those of his daughter and, for a few precious seconds, they shared this huge moment in their family's history.

Trufo turned back to the chamber and gently placed the gem into one of the empty holes. As he flicked his fingers at the key pad, the side panels of the gem chamber slowly lowered and snapped shut. He turned to face the three young detectives, who were now standing in complete amazement at what they were witnessing. 'Er, you might want to stand over there,' he said, pointing to the opposite side of the room. Eddie, Mossop and Stelvina all looked at each other and then, as one, shuffled as far away from the chamber as they could get.

When he knew they were safe, Trufo hit the bright green button on a separate key pad and turned to face the Chief Engineer.

CHAPTER 22

'Is he alive?'

The entire room filled with a deep droning sound as the Spectral Chamber sparked into life. As the powerful generators built up their intensity, the sound grew louder and louder and everybody in the room began to cover their ears. It had been a thousand years since the generators had started up and Trufo wasn't convinced they could take the surge in energy.

The noise was becoming unbearable. Trufo checked the data readout. It was off the scale. He turned to the three space detectives and shouted, 'She's going to blow. I'm going to abort,' but they couldn't hear him. And then, just as he was about to turn the generators off, a powerful emerald green beam of pure life-giving energy erupted from the gem, hitting the magnifier before slamming into Sardon's back.

The Chief Engineer's body arched backwards and he fell to the floor in a heap.

As soon as Trufo switched off the beam, the three detectives ran to Sardon. 'Is he alive?' Eddie demanded as they stood over Sardon's lifeless body. Mossop knelt down and placed the palm of his hand close to Sardon's nose. He thought he could feel a faint breath on his palm but he wasn't sure. 'Mossop, is he alive?' Eddie asked again with even more urgency.

Mossop looked up and shook his head. 'I don't know,' he replied.

Trufo walked over to the group and looked down at Sardon. He was beginning to think that he'd focussed too much power through the magnifiers. Or maybe it was just the surge of the Light being switched on that was too much for a human to take. Stelvina looked at her father, concern all over her face. 'Papa?'

Trufo sighed and puffed his cheeks out. 'I think I…' But before he could finish, he was interrupted by

Sardon's body beginning to convulse in the most horrific way. He was shaking violently, and his bulging eyes were opening and closing manically. And then, his body went into a massive spasm before collapsing into a limp, lifeless form once more.

Trufo and the detectives stood in silence with their mouths wide open.

And then, Sardon sat bolt upright.

Everybody looked at each other, scarcely able to believe what had just happened. For the first time since the Zomaks had put him into stasis, Sardon, the keeper of the Darian Light for the last 20 years, blinked. His sight was blurred so he blinked his eyes a few more times and shook his head. He could feel his chest heaving and hear his heart pumping loudly. He was aware of some sounds around him but had no idea where they were coming from or what they were. It was like he was underwater. As his sight became more focussed, he began to recognise the inside of the Spectral Chamber. As he regained his senses, the full horror of what had happened to him came flooding back. As his hearing returned he became aware that his name was being called over and over again.

'Sardon! Sardon!'

He looked up at the four faces above him. He was

soaked with sweat and his long, grey hair was stuck to his face. He tried desperately to speak. He could feel his mouth moving but he couldn't hear any words coming out. Finally, he heard himself say, 'Who are you?'

This was Eddie's territory and he wasted no time in taking control of the situation.

'Hello Sardon. I'm Eddie Poncho, this is Mossop Yate and this is Stelvina. We're from the Space Detective Agency.' Eddie placed a respectful hand on Trufo's back. 'And this is Trufo, Stelvina's father. He's the reason why you're speaking now. How are you? Can you stand up?'

Sardon wasn't sure. 'I think so. Can you help me?' he whispered. Eddie and Mossop each took an arm and gently lifted the engineer to his feet. Eddie looked at Mossop and nodded towards the seating area near the entrance to the chamber. They guided Sardon towards the green leather couch and helped him to sit down.

As they did so, Stelvina appeared with a glass of water. 'Here,' she said gently, 'take a sip of this.'

Eddie was concerned about Sardon's state of mind. He was obviously in shock, but if he had any information about where the Zomaks were hiding, they needed it quickly. Eddie signalled to Mossop and Stelvina that he wanted to speak with them in private. Leaving him to recover a little more, they walked back over to the chamber in the centre of the room.

'He's completely out of it,' Eddie said, slightly stating the obvious. 'I'm not sure we're going to get much out of him.'

Mossop was getting fidgety. It was an edginess that Eddie was very used to. It meant that Mossop wanted to get on with business. 'We don't have time for softly-softly, Eddie,' he snapped impatiently. 'I'm sure he has something to do with this. We need to know what he knows.'

Stelvina agreed with Mossop but was also concerned about Sardon. 'I know you're an expert at this stuff, Eddie. And I agree with you, Mossop, but look at him. He's completely traumatised. I'm not sure he's going to be of any use anytime soon.'

Eddie gave himself a few seconds to think before turning to Trufo, who had been busy checking the energy levels that had just been released by the Light. 'Trufo, will the Light have this effect on all of them?' he asked.

Trufo turned away from the long list of numbers that he was trying to understand and rubbed the back of his neck. 'To be honest, Eddie, I'm not sure. It looks like there was a massive power surge when I ignited the generators, which isn't really surprising when you consider they haven't been restarted for a thousand years. I had the power on a really low setting, and it's only going through one gem, of course.' He shook his head and looked across at the shivering engineer. 'Really, from these figures, he's lucky to be alive.'

Whilst her father had been speaking, Stelvina had been looking at the figures herself. She noticed that there had been a huge spike in power a second after the Light had been ignited. This had been followed by an immediate drop-off in power. 'It looks like it dumped a lot of power after the initial ignition, Papa,' she said, sounding like she knew exactly what she was talking about. Trufo looked at his daughter in amazement and had another look at the screen.

Mossop jumped in again. 'Look, I know we don't know what his state of mind is. Interrogating him could tip him over the edge but it's a price that we have to pay. He *does* know what went on here.'

'OK, Mossop,' Eddie said, having weighed up the potential dangers. 'Whatever state his brain is in, we do know that he's alive. He's out of stasis and we need to release the others as soon as possible. Maybe it was worse for him because he was the first. Trufo, can you start releasing the others?'

Trufo nodded his head before turning to his daughter. 'Can you help me, please?'

Stelvina felt a sudden surge of pride. 'Of course, Papa,' she smiled.

'Great,' said Mossop. He pointed up to the floating body with the long brown hair. 'Start with Alexa Karel. There's something about that girl…'

Whilst Trufo and Stelvina got on with the task of recalibrating the magnifier so they could bring Alexa out of stasis, Eddie and Mossop turned their attention back to Sardon. 'The old one-two?' Mossop asked Eddie with a smile.

Eddie smiled back at his old friend. 'As usual,' he replied. 'I wouldn't want to destroy your reputation as the hardest Quagoid in the Solar System!'

CHAPTER 23

'You can't wake her up.'

'Sardon! Sardon!' Mossop yelled as they walked towards the startled Chief Engineer. 'What happened here?' Sardon's eyes widened and he stared up at Mossop, whose nose was now almost touching his. Mossop barked the engineer's name again. Sardon felt panicked and shook his head. He started muttering, but nothing understandable was coming out of his mouth. Mossop tried again. 'Tell us what happened here!'

Sardon was still having trouble speaking but tried his best to answer. 'I can't remember. I mean, I can but I don't know…' Sardon paused, trying desperately to recollect anything that would stop the angry Mossop from shouting at him. 'Who are you?' he mumbled to Mossop.

Eddie grabbed Mossop's arm, the signal that it was time for a gentler approach. 'We're from the Space Detective Agency,' Eddie replied calmly, in complete contrast to the shouty approach that Mossop was adopting. 'Do you understand, Sardon?'

The engineer nodded. He was well aware of who the Space Detective Agency were. 'Yes, I do,' he replied, grateful for Eddie's more calming tones.

Eddie sat down next to the engineer whilst Mossop stood above him, trying to look as menacing as he could. 'Sardon, my name's Eddie. This is my colleague Mossop,' Eddie said, gesturing towards the snarling Quagoid. 'Would you like some more water?' Sardon nodded. Eddie looked up at Mossop and winked an eye. Mossop picked up the empty glass and went to refill it. Eddie lowered his voice to the point where he was almost whispering. He wanted to gain the engineer's trust. 'Sardon, we're here to help. We've helped you already by releasing you from stasis. But we need to know what happened here. You're in charge of the Spectral Chamber. Tell me what happened.' Eddie was trying to sound reassuring but Sardon was still looking dazed from being brought out of stasis.

Mossop returned with the fresh glass of water and handed it to Sardon. The engineer grabbed it with both of his shaking hands and took a sip. As the glass began to slip from his limp hands, Mossop reached out and clasped his own hands around Sardon's. The engineer looked up at Mossop, the fear still in his eyes. Mossop's eyes blinked from side to side. He gently released the glass from Sardon's hands and placed it on the table next to him. Sardon turned his head towards Eddie. 'I honestly don't remember much. It all happened so quickly,' he said.

Mossop wasn't impressed. When they'd first entered the chamber shortly after arriving on Dar, he was struck by the fact that Sardon had his eyes open when the other technicians' eyes were closed. Why was that? Was he treated differently? If so, why? Mossop leant forwards and placed his face close to Sardon's. 'We don't have time to waste,' he said, with a menacing look. Sardon glanced sideways at Eddie again, which prompted Mossop to bark, 'Don't look at him, I'm talking to you.' Sardon's head snapped back in fear. Deep inside, Mossop was smiling. His instincts had been right, he thought to himself. *This man is hiding something.*

Mossop decided to get straight to the point. 'How did they get the gems?' he demanded.

Tears began to form in Sardon's eyes. He looked down at the floor and said quietly, 'It's too late.'

Eddie grabbed Sardon's arm again. 'What do you mean, it's too late?' he asked. 'Did you have something to do with this, Sardon?' The Chief Engineer's shoulders began to shake. Mossop thought that he'd started to cry but when Sardon lifted his head he was laughing. Mossop reached out and grabbed Sardon's jacket but before he could speak, the room was filled with the whine of the Spectral Chamber as Trufo prepared to ignite the Light once more.

Mossop looked deep into Sardon's eyes. 'Do you know what that is?' he said calmly. Sardon had never heard the Spectral Chamber igniting because it had never gone out, but in those few seconds, he'd already guessed what the sound was. What he couldn't work out, was *how* it was making that noise. His eyes widened as Mossop's stare intensified. The Quagoid's big black eyes blinked from side to side. 'That's the sound of Alexa Karel's alarm clock,' he said menacingly.

Sardon's body began to shake and a look of fear

fell across his face. Although he tried not to, he flicked his eyes towards Alexa's floating body. 'No, no… you can't wake her up,' he stuttered.

'And why's that?' Eddie demanded. But before Sardon could answer, the deafening whine of the Light broke the silence. Eddie, Mossop and Sardon turned as one and looked towards the chamber, just in time to see Alexa Karel drop to the ground in a crumpled heap.

Eddie and Mossop ran towards Alexa and were quickly joined by Stelvina and Trufo. They were all anxious to see whether the Light would have the same effect on her as it had on Sardon. They watched in silence as Alexa immediately opened her eyes. It was relief all around. They weren't like Sardon's manic, bulging eyes. And her body wasn't convulsing either. She gently untangled her limbs, sat up and shook her head. 'Alexa!' Mossop said with concern in his voice.

Alexa looked up, her big, dark brown eyes still watery from stasis. 'Have we met?' she asked.

CHAPTER 24

'We have work to do, and you're going to help us do it.'

Alexa's eyes narrowed as she searched her memory banks for Mossop's face. Her secret search was disturbed when he knelt down next to her. 'I'm Mossop, Mossop Yate. How are you feeling?'

Alexa began to flex her fingers and wind her wrists around. 'My head feels light and my hands are numb, sort of cold, but I don't feel cold,' she replied. She looked up at Eddie, Stelvina and Trufo. Then she looked around the room and saw, for the first time, her colleagues, who were still floating in mid-air. She gasped, sharply pulling her hands up to cover her mouth. Tears filled her eyes. The sudden realisation that she'd looked the same just a few seconds earlier hit her like a Zotan wazoon falling out of a tree!

Trufo knelt down beside Mossop. 'Don't worry,' he said, trying desperately to reassure her, 'we're going to wake them all up soon. Let me get you some water.' Trufo stood up and walked over to the rest area, close to where Sardon was sitting.

Alexa lowered her hands and looked back at Mossop. 'I guess you caught them?' she asked, assuming that was the obvious explanation for why they were now able to have a conversation. Mossop blinked his eyes. 'The Zomaks? Not yet,' he replied.

Alexa was confused and looked across to the Spectral Chamber. 'But how…?'

Mossop interrupted. 'I'm sorry, Alexa, I can't tell you that yet. We need to know what you saw. He's not telling us anything.' Mossop looked towards Sardon, just in time to see him creeping towards the chamber door. 'Eddie!' Mossop shouted urgently across the room. Eddie span around and launched himself towards the escaping Chief Engineer, who was already scanning his palm over the exit panel. The door swished to one side, revealing the tall, red uniform of Captain Orval. Sardon's mouth fell open and, for a few seconds, he stood frozen to the spot as he stared up at Orval's muscle-shaped chest armour. Then he slowly lifted his head until his eyes met Orval's.

'Going somewhere, Sardon?' Orval asked sternly.

Eddie arrived at the door and thanked Orval. He grabbed Sardon's arm and pulled him back towards the seating area. 'We have work to do, Sardon, and you're going to help us do it. Now sit down,' he commanded.

Orval nodded at Eddie and followed Sardon to the bench. The engineer sat down sheepishly and looked across at Alexa. Judging by Sardon's botched escape attempt, she thought to herself, he hadn't confessed. And given that she was the only other technician to have been brought out of stasis, she figured that she'd be doing a lot of talking in the next couple of minutes.

Trufo returned with a glass of water and handed it to her. She took a few sips and quickly thought through the sequence of events that had led to her sitting on the floor of the Spectral Chamber, whilst watching her boss being eyeballed by the head of the Darian Royal Guard.

'Can you stand?' Mossop asked, offering to take the glass of water.

Alexa smiled. 'I'll try,' she replied.

Stelvina bent down and supported Alexa's right arm. 'Let me help,' she said, as Trufo offered the same assistance on Alexa's left side. The moment she got to her feet, she felt a rush of dizziness hit her. Her knees buckled as she felt herself beginning to fall back to the floor but Stelvina and Trufo took the strain and held her up. Together, they slowly walked her over to the bench opposite Sardon and lowered her down. Mossop handed her the glass and encouraged her to take another sip, which she did without once taking her eyes off the engineer. Sardon was shaking with fear, but he had an angry look in his eyes.

Eddie sat down next to Alexa and looked across at Sardon's pathetic attempt at intimidation. 'Would you rather he wasn't here?' he asked Alexa. The young Communications Officer nodded and took another sip from the glass that she was gripping tightly with both hands.

Orval was already on the case. He reached over the back of the bench and placed his large leather-gloved hand on Sardon's shoulder. 'Come with me,' he barked.

Sardon looked sideways at the hand and then looked behind him. 'I'm not going anywhere with you,' he snarled back.

Orval grabbed Sardon's other shoulder and yanked him back towards the back of the bench. 'You'll do whatever I say. Now get up,' he ordered. Reluctantly, Sardon stood up. He gave Alexa a hard stare before a sharp prod in the back from Orval told him that he was pushing his luck. 'That's enough of that,' Orval growled before lowering his tone to speak to Eddie. 'We'll be outside. Let me know when you want him back in.'

Eddie nodded his appreciation to Orval, waiting until the giant Captain and Sardon had disappeared into the corridor before speaking again. Then he turned to Alexa and asked, 'He helped them, didn't he?' Alexa nodded. Mossop smiled to himself. From the moment he'd seen Sardon in stasis, he'd known that something was different about him.

Eddie's tone became more urgent. 'We don't have much time, Alexa. I'm sure you have lots of questions but we haven't found the gems yet.'

Alexa looked horrified. 'But what about Parsus?' she asked anxiously, already knowing what the answer was probably going to be.

Mossop jumped in. 'That's where we've come from,' he replied quietly. 'It's probably too late for Parsus but we have to stop the Zomaks, and we must find the gems. Is there anything that will help us?'

Alexa took another sip of water before placing the glass on the table.

'He brought them in,' she began. 'He talked about the Zomaks all the time. He was their father's best friend and he was always moaning about the king. We could never understand that. I mean, most Darians love Brude. They have no reason to hate him.' She paused before taking a deep breath. 'Most of the people who work here don't even know who the Zomaks are,' she continued.

'But you do?' Mossop replied quickly.

'I'm a student of interplanetary history,' Alexa responded. Mossop blinked his eyes. 'It's good for my job,' she shrugged, in an attempt to explain her nerdiness.

'History's good,' Mossop smiled. Realising that she may have just met a fellow nerd, Alexa smiled back and continued.

'Anyway, he used to bang on about how Brude had betrayed this loyal family and sent these two innocent kids to prison. We just thought he was a bit mad, you know? That is until he turned up with them yesterday morning. I was preparing a report in the back office. I'd got in early and he didn't know I was in there. It was all Sardon. The Zomaks made the technicians stand in the store room whilst he removed all but one of the gems. He'd obviously been secretly working with them. He must have known that it would kill millions. His life was about keeping the Light working for our two planets. How could he take all of that away? It's horrible…' Alexa's voice trailed off.

Stelvina sat on the other side of Alexa and took hold of her hand. 'What happened? Why did he leave one gem in the chamber?' she asked. A tear trickled down Alexa's cheek. 'They brought them all out and lined them up whilst Sardon redirected the magnifier. Then he hit them all with a single beam. Their bodies all flew back as they screamed out in pain, all of them at the same time. Then they just floated away to where you see them now. He must have rewritten the program to put us all in that state.'

Everyone in the room felt silent. From Alexa's description, it wasn't hard to imagine the scene.

'How did they find you?' Mossop asked. 'They heard me crying. Sardon was furious, his cover was blown. He started yelling and ordered the Zomaks to drag me out of the room. I tried to resist but while I was fighting them he reconfigured the magnifier. The last thing I remember is him telling them to get out of the way.'

Eddie shook his head in disgust. 'They must have been planning this for years,' he said, barely able to contain his anger.

Stelvina asked the obvious next question. 'So how comes he ended up in stasis?'

Alexa didn't know but she had a theory. 'I think he offered to sacrifice himself to give them time to get away,' she said thoughtfully.

Mossop agreed. 'That makes sense,' he added in support of Alexa's deduction. 'They had to expect that Brude would cave in. As part of their ultimatum, Brude would fly to Parsus leaving them to rule Dar. They would need Sardon to operate the Light if it was to be continually turned on and off. When it was over, they could release him and no-one would be any the wiser.'

Mossop paused, looked at Alexa and blinked his big black eyes. 'Except you, of course.'

Alexa looked scared and puzzled at the same time. 'What do you mean, turn the Light on and off?' she asked.

'I'm sorry, Alexa,' Eddie responded, standing up. 'We don't have time to explain that now. Right, we need Sardon back in. I'm sure he can identify what this is a picture of.' Eddie removed the drawing from the thigh pocket of his trousers. 'Stelvina, can you take Alexa into the store room, please? Trufo, we need to free the rest of the technicians but not until we've finished with Sardon and got him out of here. Can you start working on that?'

Trufo nodded. 'Of course I can, Eddie.'

'Alexa, when we've finished with Sardon, do you feel up to giving Trufo a hand? Your colleagues are going to need a friendly face when they wake up.'

'Yes, Eddie,' Alexa smiled. 'Whatever I can do to help.'

Mossop had been quietly listening to Alexa. It all made perfect sense, but there was one thing that was puzzling him. Throughout all of this, there had been no mention of Tak Zomak. Eddie looked at Mossop and knew instantly that something was on his mind. 'Mossop?'

Mossop rubbed his chin. 'What about their father?' he asked Alexa.

'Tak?' she replied quickly.

She really did know her history, Mossop thought to himself. 'I never heard any mention of him. Is he still alive?' Mossop shrugged his shoulders. He had no idea but it was curious that in all of this, Tak's name had not been mentioned once.

Eddie was keen to get on with it. 'Right, Mossop, let's get him back in.'

CHAPTER 25

'Innocent people are dying.'

'Where is this?' Eddie asked as he thrust the drawing under Sardon's nose. The engineer scanned his eyes over the picture and instantly felt the emotion welling up inside him. It had been over 10 years since he'd seen it. He couldn't believe it still existed. He gave himself a few seconds to compose himself before looking up at Eddie. 'I don't know what you're talking about,' he said calmly.

Eddie laughed whilst Mossop shook his head in mock disbelief. 'The game's up, Sardon,' he said, still laughing. 'You must realise that. We know everything.

We know you're working with them. It's over. Brude isn't leaving Dar. He's staying right here, with his people.'

Sardon didn't say a word, he just continued to look at Eddie. Mossop decided that it was time to stop playing the aggressor and sat down next to Sardon. 'Innocent people arc dying, Sardon. You understand that, don't you? You've dedicated your whole life to maintaining the Darian Light. It's given life to millions over a thousand years. You've destroyed all that in less than two days. I can't believe that's what you wanted.'

Sardon's eyes began to fill with water.

'Eddie's right, it's over. Help us to find the Zomaks and we can put an end to this madness before Parsus dies completely.'

Mossop hesitated.

'Please…'

Sardon looked back down at the picture. A raindrop tear splattered straight onto the centre of the 10-year-old paper and immediately soaked into its bone-dry surface. Still looking down at the picture, he spoke quietly. 'Rok drew this for me.' He looked up at Eddie. 'She kept it!' Sardon put his head in his hands and started sobbing. Mossop pulled the picture from

Sardon's lap and passed it back to Eddie.

Sardon was broken. Mossop took no pleasure in watching the man crumble in front of him but the job wasn't finished yet. 'Sardon,' he said firmly, 'where are the Zomaks?'

Sardon didn't look up. Deep inside he knew he was out of options but more than that, a sense of guilt and shame was beginning to fill every fibre of his body. He was just about to speak when the chamber door swished open. Captain Orval walked in, flanked by two of his Royal Guard. Eddie looked over to Orval and held his hand up, a signal that Sardon was about to tell them what they wanted to hear. Orval stopped in his tracks and held his arms out, prompting his two lieutenants to come to an abrupt standstill.

Sardon lifted his head from his hands and looked up at Eddie. His eyes were red and swollen from the personal torment that he was now feeling.

'It's the foundations beneath the palace,' he whispered. 'There's a secret entrance. I can take you there.'

Eddie and Mossop looked at each other and then as one, looked over at Orval. All three looked as surprised as each other.

The shattered former Chief Engineer of the Spectral Chamber of the Darian Light slumped back into the couch. Shaking uncontrollably, he put his head in hands and sobbed, 'What have I done?'

CHAPTER 26

'How could anybody do that?'

'You can come out now,' Mossop announced to Stelvina and Alexa as the two guards disappeared with Sardon. 'He told us what we wanted to know. Can you believe that the picture is of the foundations of the Royal Palace? They played there as kids.'

'So Sardon betrayed them?' Alexa asked.

'He didn't expect it to get this far. I'm guessing the Zomaks felt the same. They thought the king was weak and would cave in immediately.' Mossop shook his head, barely able to comprehend the massive loss of life and devastation that had been caused by turning off the Light. 'I told him, you've spent years helping to create and maintain life…'

Mossop didn't finish the sentence. As a Quagoid, he was all about giving life. He simply couldn't understand why anybody would want to extinguish so many. Alexa reached out and touched his arm. He looked into her deep brown eyes and blinked.

'How could anybody do that?'

Alexa didn't speak. She just stared into Mossop's big eyes. Stelvina placed her arm around Alexa's shoulder and gave her a gentle squeeze. 'Are you up to helping Papa to unfreeze your friends?' she asked.

Alexa wanted nothing more than to help. 'Yes, I'm OK. I want to help,' she responded and walked purposefully over to centre of the room.

Trufo had been watching the whole episode unfold. As she walked towards him, he flashed Alexa a welcoming smile. 'You're very brave,' he told her as she arrived at the console.

Mossop and Stelvina joined Eddie and Orval in the seating area. They needed a plan, and quick. Orval spoke first.

'My Royal Guard are at your disposal, Eddie,' he offered. 'As soon as he provides the co-ordinates for the entrance to the foundations, we can leave.'

'Thank you, Captain,' Eddie responded. 'Our priority is securing those gems. Who knows what else they might be able to do with them? We don't want them jumping around the galaxy causing more carnage. I want to make absolutely sure that they have the gems with them before we attack.'

Stelvina immediately jumped in. 'I can do that,' she volunteered, looking at Mossop and then at Eddie.

'What do you mean?' Mossop asked.

'I can blend. I can blend before I go into the cave, have a look around and locate the gems. I could hide them or maybe even get them out.' Stelvina turned to face Orval, who had a look of utter confusion on his face. 'And then you can go in and get them,' she added confidently.

Eddie and Mossop exchanged glances. It was a plan.

'Can you speak and blend at the same time?' Eddie asked. Stelvina smiled. 'Well, I can but not if I'm trying to remain undetected.'

Orval couldn't contain himself any longer. 'Er, excuse me. What is blending exactly?' Stelvina suddenly realised that the tall captain had absolutely no idea what they were talking about. 'Sorry, Orval,' she apologised, slightly embarrassed. 'Er, well, I have this gift. I can sort of blend in with my surroundings. I can do it so well that to the unsuspecting eye, I sort of disappear. But I never actually disappear. It's just that you're not expecting me to be there so you don't see me.'

Orval raised his eyebrows. 'That's some gift,' he replied, somewhat impressed. 'How long can you do this for?' he asked.

Stelvina nervously bit the corner of her lip. 'As long as I've got an escape route, I can unblend without anyone ever knowing I was there.'

Orval frowned. Stelvina hadn't really answered his question. 'Yes, but what if you don't have an escape route? What then? How long, exactly?' Orval was concerned. He could tell that Stelvina was hiding something.

The young space detective looked down at the stone floor. 'Not for long,' she said quietly before looking back up at Orval. 'It takes a lot of energy and I have to unblend before…'

Silence hung in the air for a few moments before Orval filled it. 'Before what?' he asked, urgently.

'Before I become unconscious and die. But I'll unblend well before that happens,' she added, partly in an attempt to convince Orval but also to convince herself. She knew that what she was suggesting was extremely dangerous. She'd only blended twice before: once by accident, when she discovered she could do it, and once during a mission on Tizania, when she had multiple exits. In her mind, she expected the way into the cave would also be the way out… but she had no idea what things would look like until she was inside. If there wasn't another way out, things would get very sketchy.

Orval was angry, but only because he was concerned for Stelvina's safety. 'There's too much risk. My squad can end this in minutes,' he said turning to Eddie.

'Yes, of course, Captain,' Eddie responded. 'But what if the gems aren't there? Anything could happen and we may never find them or we might capture the Zomaks alive and they refuse to tell us where they've hidden them. Stelvina is putting herself at risk but that's what we do. That's why we're part of the Space Detective Agency, just as you're a soldier. We calculate the risks.'

Orval looked at Eddie with a steady eye. He gave himself a bit of thinking time before turning back to Stelvina. 'I get that,' he replied with a slightly calmer voice. 'I don't want you in there for long, Stelvina. If it's not obvious where the gems are, get the hell out of there. Let us know that you've unblended and we'll storm the cave. OK?'

Stelvina nodded. 'I don't intend to die in that cave, Orval.'

CHAPTER 27

'We must get the gems back.'

Commander Ramad stroked his silver beard thoughtfully and walked over to the window. He looked out at the thousands of twinkling stars and felt grateful for the calming effect they had on him. At heart, space was his home. It was where he felt most comfortable and, deep down, he was glad to be amongst the stars once more, even if the circumstances were very far from what he'd ever wish. The last streaks of escaping spacecraft had long since left Parsus. Below the SDA transporter, the planet was now being consumed by fire and toxic gases. There was nothing left, and even if the gems were found and the decision was made to regenerate life on Parsus, it would be a lifetime before it was safe for anyone to live there again.

Ramad turned his big shoulders back towards Eddie's image, which was being projected from the flight deck's central console. 'How confident are you that the Zomaks are in there?' he asked Eddie.

'Sardon told us that's where they're hiding,' Eddie replied. 'He's a complete wreck. They didn't expect it to pan out like this. Orval's men have taken him to the military hospital for a psychic evaluation. He's under armed guard.'

Ramad stroked his beard again.

Eddie continued with his attempts to persuade his old mentor that he should approve the plan. 'To be honest, it's going to be while before we get anything more out of him. Fortunately, he told us how to access the foundations before he lost it completely. Orval says he's completely lost his mind. He's just an empty shell now.'

Ramad nodded his head slowly. He trusted Eddie's instincts but was concerned that the Zomaks had anticipated that Brude would not co-operate and had hidden the gems. 'We must get the gems back, Eddie.

We don't want the Zomaks flying off with them,' he insisted. Eddie agreed. They really had no idea how powerful the gems were or what other use they might be put to in the future.

Time was ticking by and Eddie needed Ramad to make a decision. 'Orval's on standby, sir. We don't want the Zomaks to think the game's up and do a disappearing act. We'll be chasing them across the universe,' he said urgently.

Ramad had made his mind up. 'OK, Eddie, it's a go, but I don't want Stelvina in there for long. Blending is unpredictable so if she doesn't locate the gems quickly, I want her out of there. After that, we'll have to take our chances with Orval's squad and storm the cave.'

Eddie wanted to punch the air but held back and tightened his fist instead. 'Thank you, sir,' he said.

'OK, Eddie. We're going to head for Dar and settle into orbit. Report back when Stelvina's in the cave. Out!'

Eddie flicked at his communicator. 'Captain Orval, we're on our way down. Ramad's given us the green light.'

CHAPTER 28

'I'm not going anywhere.'

King Brude looked up at the tower of the Spectral Chamber and wondered whether he'd ever see the Darian Light shining from it again. He was also beginning to wonder what the future held for him. Throughout history, he would be remembered as the king who lost the precious gems and killed Parsus. He was the king who'd turned a thousand years of life into death within two days.

It didn't matter if the Space Detective Agency found the Zomaks and rescued the gems. He would have to stand down, and he knew it. The question was, would there be a 42nd monarch? His only child was wise beyond his years but was surely too young to take on such a task. *Maybe I can provide some transition for a few years,* he thought to himself. *That wouldn't be so bad, the people would understand that, wouldn't they? The old king passing on his knowledge?* There was a lot of work to do and Tomeke would need all the help he could get.

The thought cheered him for a brief moment but then, just as quickly, an alternative solution began to infect his brain. What if this was the end of his dynasty? What if the people of Dar decided they were sick of kings and queens? After everything that had happened, he could understand that. He knew that his son was open to a new way. The prince was close to the people and he was open to new ideas. But a government of the people…?

The shattered king allowed his shoulders to drop and his head slumped forward. He looked up again at the stars. He closed his eyes and tried to find his wife's face. After 10 long years it was becoming harder and harder to picture her in his mind. He missed her so much. Lost in his thoughts, he was disturbed by the sound of footsteps on the cold, hard stone of the palace floor. He opened his eyes and turned his head to the left. 'Tomeke,' he said quietly.

Prince Tomeke walked over to his father. He was tall and athletic, which gave him presence enough. But what you always noticed first about Tomeke was his piercing, laser-blue eyes. His long black hair was like a picture frame against his pale, almost white skin. Even if you didn't know he was a future king, he just looked like he had something to say. And you knew that something that would be worth listening to.

When he reached his father, Tomeke spoke calmly and with authority. Brude was taking Sardon's betrayal and the devastation on Parsus badly. Tomeke understood the pain his father was feeling but deep down, he was pleased to have the opportunity to prove that he could play a bigger part in the affairs of his planet, particularly at its time of greatest need.

'They're on their way, Papa,' he reported to the king. 'It's the SDA's mission but Captain Orval is co-leading with Poncho. I've insisted on that.' He paused and placed a hand on his father's shoulder. 'We have to think about getting you out of here. This attack is going to take place directly beneath us.'

The old king turned around and looked deeply into his son's piercing blue eyes. He pulled his shoulders back and lifted his chin up. 'I'm not going anywhere,' he said firmly.

CHAPTER 29

'I'm a bit scared.'

The four sinister-looking assault vehicles came to a sudden standstill, swiftly followed by Eddie and Mossop on their power-bikes. As the doors of the black vehicles whirred open, Darian Guardsmen spilled out and took up offensive positions opposite the mass of green vegetation. As Eddie and Mossop walked towards the lead vehicle, they were met by Orval and Stelvina, who had travelled with the tall captain. Orval flicked his fingers in the direction of four of the guards and signalled for them to start searching for the entrance of the cave. 'These are the co-ordinates Sardon gave us,' Orval said to Eddie.

'Let's hope he hasn't tricked us,' Eddie replied unconvincingly.

The sound of the late afternoon breeze was disturbed by rustling as the red-uniformed guards set about moving branches and leaves. Eddie and Orval moved closer to get a better look, but Mossop walked over to Stelvina and stood by her side. He nudged her playfully with his shoulder. 'How are you doing?' he asked in as light-hearted a tone as he could manage.

Stelvina smiled weakly. 'To be honest, Mossop, I'm a bit scared.'

Mossop smiled back. 'Of course you are. You should be. That's what will keep you sharp… and keep you safe.'

The Quagoid was just about to offer some more confidence-building words when he was interrupted by a guard shouting, 'Sir!'

Mossop nudged Stelvina again and smiled reassuringly. 'Game on!' he whispered, calmly. Stelvina puffed her cheeks out and swallowed deeply.

Eddie Poncho had now joined his fellow space detectives. 'You'll be fine, Stelvina,' he offered, attempting to reassure her some more. 'Remember, if you can't see the gems get the hell out of there, OK?'

Suddenly, the strong-minded young woman from the mountains felt vulnerable. She looked into Mossop's big black eyes and forced herself to smile. Then she walked over and joined Orval at the newly revealed tunnel door.

Orval gave the order for one of his guards to open the door, which he did slowly. The other guards gripped their weapons tighter as the door creaked, which prompted the soldier to open it even more slowly. When the door was fully opened, Orval passed Stelvina a torch. 'Good luck,' he said quietly, before adding, 'You've got five minutes, maximum. After that we're coming in.'

'Thank you, Captain. I'll hit my communicator three times when I see the gems.'

Orval nodded. He understood how much courage it was taking for Stelvina to do what she was doing. He admired her for it but now was not the time for such sentimentality. Stelvina needed to get in there and get the job done.

Stelvina turned the torch on, aimed its beam at the dusty ground and slowly walked through the door. As she disappeared into the darkness, Orval looked over towards Eddie. 'I'm not happy with this,' he said with a worried look on his face.

Stelvina made her way slowly down the dark tunnel, not wanting to make any noises that would give her presence away to the Zomaks. She was careful to keep the beam of light pointing at the floor. The tunnel was cold and smelled damp. As she walked, she ran her other hand over the tunnel wall. She'd expected it to look old and roughly dug, but she could feel that the walls were smooth and well-engineered. She quickly realised the path she was walking on was also smooth and well-made. Luckily for her, the layer of dust that covered the path cushioned her bootsteps against the hard floor. As she moved the torch from side to side across the path, she could clearly see more footsteps. She stopped for a moment and felt an immediate burst of adrenaline surge through her body. *Someone has been down here very recently,* she thought to herself. She breathed out gently and continued to walk through the tunnel's dim light.

As she looked up from the path, she suddenly stopped dead in her tracks. Up ahead she could see a small shard of light, which cut through the dusty darkness. She immediately turned the torch off and slowly started walking again. As she got nearer to the light, it became obvious that it was coming through a half-open door. She stood still and put the torch into a pouch on the side of her belt.

It was time to blend.

Stelvina closed her eyes and leant back onto the cold, hard stone. She let her arms fall loosely by her sides and spread the palms of her hands open. Then, pointing her palms backwards, she pushed the tips of her fingers against the stone. As her hands touched the wall, she relaxed her shoulders and gently moved her head back until it also came into contact with the wall. She focussed her breathing, taking slow deep breaths in, and long controlled breaths out. As she did so, she imagined herself sinking into the wall, becoming at one with it. And then, when she could no longer feel the wall through her fingertips, she knew that the blend had happened. She was now so linked to her surroundings that it was almost impossible to see her.

Stelvina released herself from the wall and walked towards the light. Within a few steps, she had carefully edged her way through the half-open door. And there she stood, in the vast cave, looking straight at Bak and Rok Zomak.

CHAPTER 30

'I've had enough.'

Bak Zomak spun around from the bank of screens in front of him and stared straight at Stelvina. She froze instantly and held her breath. Bak's eyes lasered in on hers. His stare was so intense that she felt certain he could see her. His eyelids narrowed, as if he was straining to see something in the distance. She only had limited experience of blending but she knew that he couldn't see her. And judging by the look on Bak's face, he certainly couldn't. But that stare. What could he see? He was looking straight at her. Her heart was pounding so hard against her ribcage that she was afraid he'd hear it beating. She was trying desperately to control her breathing but her heart-rate just wouldn't come down.

Gradually, her heart-rate began to slow and she began to relax a bit. She knew that severe stress could cause her to unblend, which given her situation, would be very dangerous.

Rok was now feeling really uneasy about her older brother, and this sudden staring at the cave wall wasn't making her feel any better about things. 'What's wrong? What are you looking at?' Rok asked. Bak held a hand out towards Rok and told her to be quiet, which agitated Rok even more. 'Bak, what the hell? You're really freaking me out,' Rok shouted urgently, but the elder Zomak ignored her. He slowly walked over to where Stelvina was standing and stopped right in front of her. His eyes: they were so intense that it felt like he was trying to unpick her mind, work out her inner secrets. She gulped as quietly as she could and felt a little sigh of relief that it had coincided with Rok shouting Bak's name again. The sound of Rok's voice brought Bak out of his trance and he finally blinked. He shook his head twice to wake himself, walked over to the wooden door and kicked it shut.

Stelvina threw a hand up to her mouth as she tried to stop the gasp from jumping out. A sudden wave of terror filled her body as the terrible truth hit her. She was now trapped in the palace's foundations, and she would not be able to unblend without the Zomaks knowing she was there.

Her eyes moved from the closed door to Bak as he breezed past her on his way back to the screens. 'What was all that about?' Rok asked.

'I thought I saw something. I'm starting to feel very uneasy in here,' Bak replied.

Rok threw her arms up sarcastically. 'Oh, really? That's what I've been telling you. Brude isn't going anywhere, we've just heard him say that.' Rok was angry now and pointed towards the door and the invisible space detective.

'You've shut the door but we need to get out of here. I'm telling you, Bak, you've lost it. It's over. There are no more pictures from Parsus. We've killed it, it's dead. We have to get out now, while we still can. It's not going to be easy to get off this planet, you know.'

A flicker of agreement finally appeared on Bak's face. Perhaps Rok was right. Perhaps they had over-played their hand. Could he really have misjudged this so badly? 'What about the gems?' he asked, pointing at the black carbonite case on the table in front of them. Stelvina's eyes locked onto the case and her heart started pounding again.

The gems are here… and they're safe. Realising that she was holding her breath again, she breathed out slowly. Her eyes flicked around the cave, looking for a possible place to hide. Her mind was in overdrive as she tried to work out how she could get the gems away from the Zomaks.

'I don't care about those anymore,' Rok barked back at her brother. 'It's over. How long before they find us? You have no plan for getting off this stupid planet, do you? You think you're so clever. After what we've done, they're going to hunt us down. They won't stop. We're going to be on the run forever.'

Bak was becoming more than a little irritated by his younger sister's aggression and pointed angrily at her. 'Shut up, Rok. I knew you didn't have the stomach for this. The only person who knows we're here is Sardon, and he won't be waking up any time soon.' But Rok wasn't interested in listening to her brother anymore. Guilt was beginning to take control of her, but Bak seemed in complete denial. Or was it that he simply didn't care about what they'd done, the people they'd killed?

'I've had enough,' Rok yelled. 'I'm getting out of here.' And with that, she headed towards the door.

Stelvina stood in amazement at what she was witnessing. The Zomaks' plan had fallen apart and their relationship was unravelling in front of her. They'd turned on each other like a pack of wild animals. As Rok walked past Stelvina on her way to the door, Bak launched himself towards his sister. Stelvina saw her chance. The gems were now completely unguarded. She ran towards the table but immediately felt the lightness in her head. She looked behind her, just in time to see Bak jump on his sister, bringing the pair crashing to the ground. She grabbed the carbonite case, but as soon as she picked it up the sense of dizziness completely overcame her. She moved slowly towards the base of one of the huge stone arches, hoping to hide herself behind it, but before she could reach her intended target she fell to the floor with a loud thud.

Bak and Rok both froze and looked towards the arch, their mouths wide open as they watched Stelvina's silent and crumpled body appear in front of them.

CHAPTER 31

'You mean she's…?'

Rok knelt beside the lifeless form. She looked over towards the black case that had crashed against the base of the arch and then looked back at Stelvina. Bak walked over and knelt down on the other side of the young space detective. 'Who the hell is she?' Rok said with a shaky voice. She'd been unnerved by her elder brother's increasingly erratic behaviour, but this was on another level altogether. She was really frightened now. This young woman had got into the cave and tried to take the gems, and they didn't even know she was there. Bak pulled Stelvina's white hood away from the side of her face. He placed the palm of his hand near her nose, pulling it away after a few short moments.

'What is it?' Rok asked urgently.

Bak smiled and looked back at the tunnel door. 'I knew I'd seen something,' he smiled with quiet satisfaction.

Rok was in a complete panic now. 'Is she OK?' she stuttered.

Bak shook his head. 'I don't think so.'

'You mean she's…'

Bak interrupted before Rok could finish the sentence. 'I don't know, Rok. Stop asking me questions. I need to think.'

'Think?' Rok shouted at her brother. 'It's too late for that.'

She stood up and looked down at Bak. Her whole body was throbbing with emotion, which was in complete contrast to her brother's apparent calmness. 'You're crazy if you think she came here alone,' she continued. 'In fact, I think you're just crazy. I'm getting out of here.'

Rok had made her mind up. Her brother had lost all sense of reality and she wanted no further part in his horrendous plan: a plan that had failed miserably and had resulted in death and carnage on a scale that Rok had never imagined possible. She walked towards the tunnel door but was forced to stop dead in her tracks when three red-uniformed soldiers burst through the door and pointed their blasters straight at her face. The younger Zomak froze as more heavily armed soldiers streamed into the cave and surrounded her. She looked over to Bak, just in time to see him dragging Stelvina's body towards the arch. 'Stop right there, Zomak,' came the surprise command behind Bak. 'I've got a Trident Blaster pointing right at your head. Put her down… gently.'

Bak loosened his grip from under Stelvina's arms and gently lowered her to the ground. His eyes widened as they met Rok, whose own eyes were beginning to fill with tears. 'Turn around… slowly,' came the second command. Bak held his arms out and slowly turned around. His eyes focused on the three holes at the end of the trident, before following the barrel of the blaster down to the thatch of floppy blonde hair at the other end. Eddie smiled and nodded at Bak. 'This little game is over,' he said calmly.

Orval commanded some of his Royal Guard to arrest the Zomaks, then he walked over and picked up the case of gems. He knelt down next to Stelvina's body and felt for a pulse. 'She's gone,' he said to no-one in particular. He looked up at his second-in-command. 'Get them out of my sight,' he snapped. 'And put them in separate cells.'

'Yes, sir,' came the immediate reply.

Eddie prodded Bak in the chest with the end of his trident. 'Move,' he ordered, glancing towards the approaching soldiers.

Bak smiled and nodded slowly back at Eddie. He narrowed his eyes in a way that suggested he knew something that Eddie didn't and said, 'I'll be seeing you again.'

Eddie frowned back, jabbing Bak in the chest again with his Trident Blaster. 'Not where you're going,' he smiled.

Bak arched his back as his arms were pulled backwards by a guard, who quickly snapped a pair of plasma cuffs on his wrists. The guard grabbed Bak's arm and began to drag him away, but even as he walked away from Eddie he kept his eyes locked on the space detective. Rok was the first to be led down the tunnel, her head bowed in shame. Bak didn't even acknowledge his sister. He just stood there defiantly, fixing an icy stare on Eddie.

Orval had seen enough and walked over to Bak,

which brought the staring competition to an abrupt end. The tall captain flicked his head, and Bak Zomak was led into the dark tunnel.

CHAPTER 32

'It's my choice.'

Mossop knelt down besides Stelvina and placed a hand gently on her shoulder. Orval walked over, shaking his head. 'I knew this was a bad idea,' he said.

Mossop looked up at Eddie and blinked his big black eyes from side to side. 'I can save her,' he said quietly.

Eddie frowned. 'What?'

Orval's expression turned from sadness to confusion as he tried to absorb Mossop's words. 'What are you talking about? She's dead, Mossop,' Orval said firmly.

Mossop smiled to himself. The elders were right: when the moment came, you didn't give it a second thought. You just knew it was the right thing to do. 'I don't have time to explain, and she doesn't have much time at all,' Mossop replied urgently. 'We need to get her lying face-up. Eddie, can you help Orval, please? I have to get myself ready.'

Eddie threw his trident against the wall and grabbed his friend's arm. 'What's going on, Mossop?' he demanded.

'I'm going to bring her back, Eddie,' the Quagoid replied calmly. 'It's the right thing to do.'

Eddie wasn't so sure and began shaking Mossop's arm as he spoke. 'But what if it doesn't work? What if *you* don't come back?'

Eddie's ever-tightening grip was beginning to hurt, so Mossop grabbed his hand and prised it from his arm. He completely understood his friend's fears but there was nothing to discuss. 'We don't have time for this, Eddie,' he replied with a bit more urgency. 'It's my choice.'

Eddie looked into Mossop's big eyes. Deep down, he knew he wasn't going to talk him out of it. He didn't understand why he was trying, but he knew that Mossop wasn't going to change his mind. He offered the faintest of smiles, which prompted Mossop to put a hand on one of Eddie's shoulders. 'I'll be OK,' he said reassuringly. 'Now, please, help Orval for me.'

Eddie grabbed Mossop's hand and squeezed it tightly. 'Don't leave me, Mossop,' he said quietly before allowing his friends hand to fall from his. Eddie turned around and asked Orval to help him move Stelvina onto her back. As they walked towards her limp body, Orval, who had been listening quietly to the exchange between Eddie and Mossop whispered, 'What the hell's going on?'

Eddie glanced at Mossop. 'We're about to see something for the first, and hopefully last time. Now, help me get her straight.' They turned Stelvina over as gently as they possibly could. Then Eddie straightened her legs and arms, whilst Orval slowly lowered her head to the stony floor.

As Stelvina was being moved, Mossop stood against the wall of the cave, closed his eyes and listened to the sound of his breathing. He'd always thought that if the time came, he'd be a nervous wreck but he actually felt the opposite. A strange sense of calm had fallen across his body. He listened to the sound of his breathing going in and out and told himself to relax. First, he allowed his head to gently drop forwards. This was followed by his shoulders. As he did so, he began to feel his arms and legs getting heavier and heavier. He slowly lifted his head and instinctively knew that he was ready. He opened his eyes and looked down at Stelvina. Eddie and Orval had already stepped away and were standing by the bank of screens, which Orval had turned off.

Mossop knelt down besides Stelvina's head and placed his fingertips on each of Stelvina's temples. He touched the temples briefly before moving his hands away.

So much for the test run...

He took a long, deep breath, closed his eyes again and emptied his mind once more. Then he moved his hands back towards Stelvina's head and gently made contact with her temples for a second time.

Orval leant towards Eddie and whispered, 'Is he doing what I think he his?'

Eddie nodded. 'He's a Quagoid!'

Orval raised his eyebrows. That explained it. He'd heard about the mysterious species. They existed throughout the universe but weren't indigenous to any particular planet or species. They are a subspecies, and no-one really understands where their genetic line started. Zota is known as a planet that Quagoids feel a connection with. It's a place where they feel understood, where they feel a belonging. But they're a secretive people who are extremely humble about their magical gift.

You never knew a Quagoid by the way they looked. Mossop was a Zotan who, by genetic make-up, also happened to be a Quagoid. And you never heard a Quagoid boasting about bringing someone back to life. That wouldn't be right. That wasn't the way it was done.

Orval had never knowingly met a Quagoid and now here he was, below the palace that he'd protected with such dedication, about to witness one giving life back to his young friend.

'Has he done this before?' Eddie felt sure that Mossop would have told him if he had. He was sure that he hadn't but it all seemed so natural to Mossop. But Eddie was completely hypnotised by the scene in front of him and didn't answer Orval.

Mossop went deeper and deeper into himself as he tried to focus all of his energy through his fingertips and into Stelvina's body. He could feel how heavy and lifeless she was. Her body was like a stone wall, blocking the life-force that he was trying to give her. It was the tell-tale sign that she only had a few moments left before her brain shut down completely. Mossop could feel the sense of panic beginning to grip him. He instinctively knew that if the Trace didn't begin in the next few seconds, then it would be too late for Stelvina and too late for him.

Somehow, he found the strength to focus even more and began to feel some lightness returning to Stelvina's body. Just when he thought he couldn't hold on for any longer, the ghostly Echoes of both him and Stelvina rose out of their bodies and floated in mid-air. The mouths of everyone who was in the cave opened in amazement.

Mossop's hands began to shake as the remaining bits of energy passed into Stelvina's body, making him feel weaker and weaker. His head was spinning and he felt so dizzy that he thought he would pass out at any moment. He clenched his teeth as the two Echoes floated over to the table of screens. Moving as one now, they stopped at the table, freezing at the point in time when Stelvina grabbed the black carbonite case containing the Gems of Dar.

Just as he thought he wouldn't be able to take any more, a sharp searing pain attacked his brain.

Instinctively, he threw his hands up to his head and screamed out in agony. As he did so, the Echoes exploded in a flash of bright blue light, vanishing almost immediately.

'Mossop!' Eddie shouted, throwing himself towards his friend. In an attempt to support him Eddie grabbed Mossop around his body, just in time to stop him from slumping to the floor.

'Mossop,' Eddie cried again, but there was no reply from the Quagoid. He was unconscious and barely breathing.

Orval came over and helped Eddie to lay Mossop gently on the floor. 'What happens now?' he asked.

Eddie wiped his wet eyes and tried to contain the panic he felt inside. 'I'm not sure,' he replied. 'Hopefully, he wakes up.'

'Eddie...'

Eddie and Orval looked at each other and looked back towards Stelvina. Her eyes were open and she was looking up at the roof of the cave. They both leant over so that Stelvina could see their faces. 'Hello,' Eddie smiled, 'we thought we'd lost you.' He knelt down by her side and held her hand. 'How do you feel?' he asked.

Stelvina tried to lift her head but couldn't. 'I can't feel anything. I can't move. Eddie, I'm really scared.'

Eddie tried to reassure her by squeezing her hand gently, but Stelvina didn't react. He squeezed it again, quite a bit harder this time, but she didn't even flinch. He glanced up at Orval and they shared a worried look. Then he looked across at Mossop, who was still lying motionless.

'The gems…' Stelvina gasped, suddenly remembering the reason why she was lying in this damp cave.

Orval responded with a calm smile. 'We have them… and the Zomaks. It's over.'

Stelvina flicked her eyes in his direction and smiled. Then she frowned. Someone was missing. 'Where's the Quagoid?' she asked urgently, feeling herself overcome with a wave of panic.

She knew that she'd over-blended. She should be dead, but she wasn't and that could only mean one thing. She flicked her eyes between Eddie and Orval but neither responded. Feeling her anxiety building she demanded that someone give her an answer. Eddie nodded his head in Mossop's direction. 'He's over there. He's unconscious. Well, we think he is.' Instinctively, Stelvina raised her head so that she could see Mossop.

She *could* move.

Her concern for Mossop was briefly replaced by joy as she realised that her body was coming back to life. Orval placed a hand on her shoulder and gently guided her head back down so that it was lying on the floor of the cave. 'Not so fast,' he said, 'let it happen naturally.'

Stelvina smiled at the tall captain. 'I felt that,' she responded, immediately embarrassed by what she'd just said. Her eyes moved slowly away from Orval's and met Eddie's. 'Mossop? Did he Trace?' She didn't need to ask the question, she already knew the answer.

Eddie nodded. 'He didn't think twice.'

Stelvina blinked her emerald green eyes a couple of times and her mouth began to judder as a trickle of water made its way down her cheek. She was trying to understand what had happened. She had nearly died, and Mossop had decided to sacrifice some of his own life to save hers.

Suddenly, a mighty roar echoed around the cave. It bounced off the vast walls and great stone arches.

Eddie and Orval spun around and there was Mossop Yate: sitting bolt upright and staring down at the pile of bright blue goo that now covered his legs. He wiped the splashes from his mouth and shook his head. Then, turning to look at Eddie and Orval's astonished faces said, 'I don't suppose you have any water, do you?'

Eddie walked over and looked down at the blue mess. It looked like Mossop had chucked a whole glass of Baboo over himself. He laughed as he knelt down and put an arm around his old friend's shoulder. 'You're in a complete mess, mate,' he said, tears in his eyes once more.

Mossop blinked his eyes from side to side and leant forwards so that his forehead was touching Eddie's. 'I didn't know if I'd survive,' he said quietly.

Eddie squeezed his friend and pushed his forehead even more firmly into Mossop's. 'It was incredible to watch,' he said. 'You did an amazing thing. She's alive.'

Mossop moved his head back and blinked. Behind them, Orval was carefully helping Stelvina to her feet.

'Feel ready to stand up?' Eddie asked. Mossop nodded, and with Eddie's help, got to his feet. When he turned around, Stelvina was standing in front of him. She looked at his big eyes, then down at the blue gunk that was dripping from his trousers and onto his boots. She looked back up and wiped her eyes, searching for the right words. She lifted a hand and placed it gently on Mossop's cheek. He closed his eyes for a few brief moments. Some Quagoids never got to experience what he'd just been through. Some chose not to. He knew that he'd never be the same again. He also knew what it meant to Stelvina. She didn't need to say anything, and he didn't need her to.

He opened his eyes and smiled at the pale, white-dressed figure in front of him. Even in the dim light of the cave, her green eyes seemed brighter than usual. The two space detectives shared a smile. 'I'm glad you're OK,' Mossop whispered.

'I'm glad *you're* OK,' Stelvina replied. 'Now, don't *ever* do that again!'

CHAPTER 33

'Too many people have died.'

Eddie walked up to the large open doors of the palace's Great Hall and stopped. He looked over to the large window on his right and smiled at the clear bright sky. Just a few moments earlier, he'd been outside feeling the warmth of the early summer sun on his face. As he made his way over from the spaceport, he'd decided to stop in the garden. He sat under the giant froo tree and spent a few quiet moments thinking about home. He thought about the horrific death and destruction that Sardon and the Zomaks had brought to his planet, and he sat there shivering as the thought hit him that he'd probably never set foot on Parsus again.

He'd had enough of Dar and its fragile life-giving powers. He just wanted to be back in the air now. There was a new life to start on a new planet and he just wanted to get on with it. The job was done. It was time to move on to the next one.

Prince Tomeke was holding court with Trufo and Stelvina. King Brude was there, a fatherly hand on his son's shoulder, smiling and proud but slightly detached. Brude's reign was coming to an end and he knew it. Despite the smiles, it was written all over his face, Eddie thought to himself. It was Tomeke who would lead Dar and Parsus out of the darkness and here, right in front of him, the transition was taking place.

Over by the window, Mossop and Alexa chatted happily over a glass of Baboo. Eddie smiled to himself once more. Before checking in with Commander Ramad, his final job had been to purchase as many froo bars as he could lay his hands on. 'We won't be coming back here for a while,' Mossop had said. Eddie had spent a small fortune on the bars and knew how excited his old friend would be when he saw them. Nobody ate a froo bar quite like Mossop Yate. In fact, he usually got so much of it on his face it was a wonder he ever got to taste one!

The Quagoid caught sight of Eddie and held his half-empty glass up by way of a greeting. Eddie smiled and flicked his head backwards. They had a rendezvous with the transporter, it was time to go.

'Eddie Poncho!'

The tall athletic figure of Prince Tomeke walked towards Eddie with his palms outstretched in the traditional Parsian way. Eddie smiled back and met Tomeke halfway. 'We have a lot to thank you all for. You've given us a future,' he said before turning to face his father. 'And you've given us much to think about.'

Brude smiled weakly. He had his own questions to answer, he knew that. Tomeke wanted a more open system of government on Dar, one where the Royal Family had less involvement in the day-to-day running of the planet. Brude's way was the old way. It was the price his family would have to pay and Tomeke was the right person to take things forward.

'Thank you for all your help, Highness,' Eddie responded cheerfully. 'I'm sorry that we couldn't have found the gems sooner. It doesn't feel like we've achieved much. Too many people have died.'

The future king of Dar let his arms fall to his sides. 'You're right of course, Eddie. We have many things to do. As we speak, Bak Zomak is on his way back to the prison planet of Cabor. He is extremely dangerous and must be kept separated from his sister. Rok will face trial. Her fate will be decided by the people of Dar. She has remorse, unlike her brother, but she must face the consequences for the destruction that she has brought to these beautiful, peaceful planets. Above all, they must be kept apart for the rest of their lives.'

'And what about Sardon?' Stelvina demanded, her green eyes ablaze with anger.

Tomeke did not hesitate with his answer. 'Sardon has betrayed us all. He has betrayed everything that our society has stood for. He has re-written a thousand years of Darian history and, when the time comes, he will be judged. But right now, he is an empty shell. He is unable to speak for himself or account for his actions. He will remain under house arrest until he is considered able to stand trial.'

Tomeke paused for a moment and looked deeply into Stelvina's eyes. 'Do you agree, Stelvina?'

Stelvina gave herself a moment to think. She was finding it incredibly difficult to contain her emotions, and everybody in the room knew it. For her family, this had been personal. She'd discovered that she had a connection to the magical gems that would live with her forever. It was a connection that she would pass on to her children, and they would pass it on to their own. This mission had almost taken her life. It was not easy to show any compassion towards Sardon.

Finally, she nodded in agreement. 'Yes, it's the right thing to do.' Tomeke smiled gently. He understood how difficult it had been for Stelvina to say that.

As if to draw a line under what had just happened, the prince clapped his hands loudly. 'So, I think you have some things to discuss before you leave,' he said mysteriously. Eddie frowned and looked across to Mossop and Alexa, just in time to see Mossop blink his eyes from side to side. This made Eddie nervous.

Brude joined his son. 'We owe you all a great debt,' he said gently. 'Thank you, you will always be welcome on Dar.'

Eddie bowed his head in respect before looking up at the King of Dar. 'Thank you, Majesty. Good luck with rebuilding my planet. Please take good care of it.'

Brude bowed his head in the same way that Eddie had. 'We shall, I promise you,' he said. And with that, Brude and Tomeke left the Great Hall.

Eddie turned to face his Quagoid friend. 'Mossop?' he questioned, with suspicion in his voice.

'Actually, it's me, Eddie,' Stelvina answered.

Eddie frowned again. 'What is it, Stelvina?'

Stelvina looked across to her father and smiled. 'I've spoken to Ramad,' she began, 'and I've decided to stay here and help Papa get the Darian Light up-and-running again.' She grabbed her father's hand and gave it a squeeze. 'We've got a planet to make. I kind of feel like it was what I was born for.'

Eddie laughed. In his head, he'd thought that Mossop had decided to stay so he was somewhat relieved to hear Stelvina's news. 'I think that's great,' he said truthfully before turning to Trufo. 'You must be pleased to have your daughter back, Trufo?' The big mountain man had tears in his eyes and could do nothing but nod his head in agreement.

'Thank you both for everything,' Eddie continued. 'Trufo, we couldn't have done this without you. Stelvina, you've been amazing. The SDA will miss you.'

Stelvina smiled back. 'It wasn't a hard decision. This job kills me!'

The laughter was cut short by Mossop. 'There is one more thing,' he said. Eddie frowned again. 'We have a vacancy, right?'

Eddie's frown quickly disappeared as he immediately

realised where Mossop was going with this. 'Er, I guess so,' he replied, flicking his eyes in Alexa's direction.

'Alexa?' Mossop urged, encouraging her to step forward. The young Communications Officer took a deep breath.

'There's nothing left for me here now,' she said, her voice shaking with nerves. 'I need a new home. I need a new family. I want to come with you. Mossop has agreed to nominate me for the academy and be my mentor.'

Eddie smiled and gave his old friend a wink before turning back to Alexa. 'You couldn't wish for anyone better,' he said proudly.

Mossop clapped his hands together. 'Excellent, that's sorted,' he said with a big smile. 'So, where are we going?'

Eddie Poncho moved closer to Mossop and placed a hand on his shoulder. 'I've just spoken with Commander Ramad.' He paused for a moment, trying to hold back the emotion that was beginning to well up inside him. Then he squeezed his friend's shoulder.

'Home, Mossop. You're going home.'

THE END

ABOUT THE AUTHOR

Martin Street grew up watching science-fiction films and TV programmes: from the original Star Trek TV series and Space 1999 to Star Wars and Alien, he fell in love with the bold new worlds and the galaxies, far, far away.

In later life, he shared this interest with his son when they co-wrote a short science-fiction story for his school homework. Inspired and influenced by these adventures in the stars, and by his son's growing interest in science-fiction, Martin has a passion for creating his own worlds and introducing them to a new generation.

19867282R00115

Printed in Great Britain
by Amazon